LIKE MIST
OVER THE EYES

LIKE MIST
OVER THE EYES

by Thea van Diepen

To Mom,
because some of our arguments made it into this book
(in one form or another)
and I thought I should apologize in advance.
Sorry.

Map of Evinad
by Adren

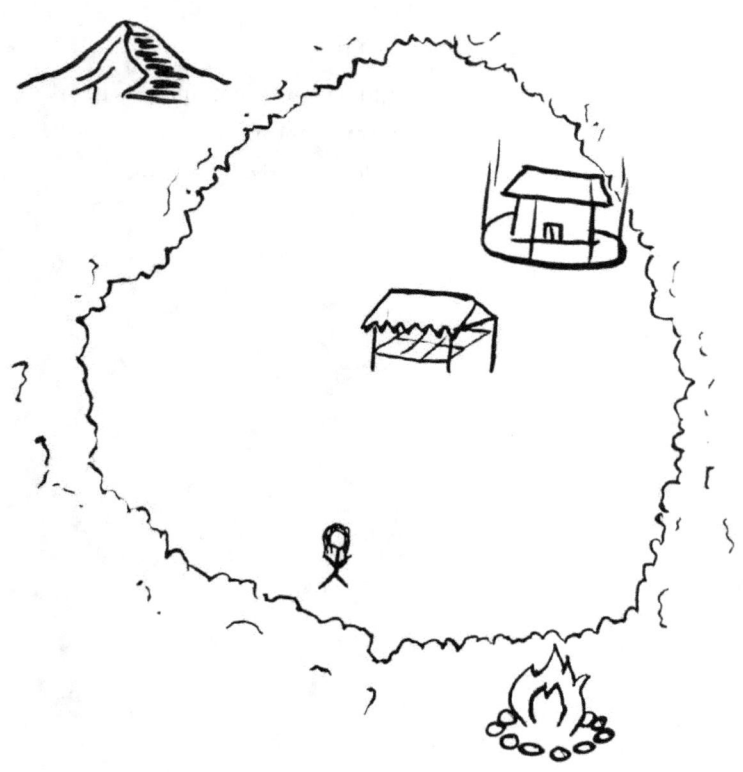

ONE

As the blade began to describe an elegant arc, Adren hoped that, this time, it wouldn't hit. But the stroke had been predestined, and it fell down and down and through and her mind was again ablaze with pain.

Again? Had this happened before?

Images sometimes rose from her mind, subsiding only to leave behind the fragments her magic could scrape from them. But this—

It wouldn't leave.

It wouldn't stop hurting.

Nadin spoke and his voice echoed in the air as the pain shot down to Adren's stomach and she doubled over out of reflex. She could feel him come against her, hold her against falling, his words going through her in a flowing arrhythmia. Instead of clutching herself, like she wanted to do, she clawed at him until he stopped talking and stood rigid, the feel of his body a vapour across the firestorm within her.

"I remember," Adren said. "I remember, I remember, I remember, I remember..." She couldn't stop herself.

"Adren!" Nadin's voice, cracked through with fear, shattered the fog within her. The forest wavered into focus again. "Adren, what happened?" Realizing how closely he held her, she pushed away and tried to stand still despite how her legs wobbled.

"A sword..." She closed her eyes.

"What else?"

She waved at him to shut up; the memory was fading fast. A sword and... and... down it went, sucked back into the darkness. Everything into the darkness.

"Did you have to hold me so saintsall tight?" Adren rubbed her forehead to soothe its lingering ache. If only her chest weren't so tight.

"Sorry." Nadin's head drooped. "I think you drew blood this time." He pulled up his sleeve and showed her the red strips.

Adren winced.

"Do you remember anything else besides the sword?" He gingerly replaced the sleeve, then took off his pack and started rummaging through it. A wind shook the aspens; a few of their leaves fell, adding to the growing carpet of yellow and orange.

"No. I don't even remember that." It was difficult, filling her lungs and letting out the air again. She prayed to all the saints that Nadin could hear nothing amiss in her voice even as she hoped he did, that he would make her say all the truth that he didn't know.

"You need to get better help than me about this. Are we near that village yet?" After a quick shake of his pack, Nadin sighed and put it back down. "Damn. I think I'm out of bandages."

"No, no." Her breath sped up and fear escaped in a tendril through the connection at the back of her mind before she could hold it down. "I don't need to go in."

"We need meat, too," he said. "We've been—"

The fear flipped within her, pressing against the walls of her chest and threatening to break past her control. "Fine! Fine. Go. It's just a short walk that way." She waved to her right and then sat, almost shaking with the effort it took to hold everything in. *Don't go through yet, not while he's still here.*

"Are you—?"

"Just go! I'll wait."

And, with a rustling of leaves, he did. Adren listened to his footsteps crash across the soundscape of the forest. Insects whirred, birds sang, other animals pattered through the trees, and Nadin overwhelmed them all. Saints, why did humans always have to be so loud? But it soon faded. She checked over her shoulder and found nothing but the marks of his passing. Taking off her pack, she held her knees to her chest and let her fear find the connection and pass through. Alarm came back in response, followed by motion.

Shafts of sunlight danced across the ground as the trees swayed in a breeze Adren could not feel. She rocked a bit without realizing, hands tight against her shins, listening, listening...

That sense of motion came with a location, and that location neared and neared until the crack of twigs and swish of branches against hide announced the arrival of a white, four-legged beast, its spiral horn gleaming like pearl when it caught the sun. Adren stood at once and, as she wrapped her arms around the unicorn's neck, she wept.

The unicorn nuzzled her, its confusion leaking through into her mind, but not so strong as to overpower its desire to comfort.

How many of these episodes had there been now? Ever since the town of Watorej, where she and Nadin had first met, since the potion maker had tried to bind her with magic but broke open a secret part of her mind instead.

The first episode had been in the night and she had woken Nadin with her screaming. Apparently, she'd said a lot more about what she'd seen that time, but he'd been so shaken that he couldn't make any sense of it. She had frightened him so much with her ranting that he'd thrown his pack at her, finally bringing her to her senses. After that first time, the only thing she'd been able to tell him before she forgot what she'd remembered was that there had been a sword, although she could never remember telling him so. Even the magic that now shivered through her veins couldn't hold back any fragments from attacks, like it sometimes did with the images that would surface at other times.

For the first while, she'd expected the episodes to slow and stop. Instead, they'd started coming more and more often. Now, as she clung to the unicorn, overcome with all the emotions of the past three weeks, she couldn't help but think that they would never stop.

"What's happening to me?" she asked the unicorn without expecting an answer. Unicorns could understand speech and communicate back, but this one had a sort of insanity that kept it at the level of a neurotic animal. Still, it was comforting to know that it listened. "What if this becomes permanent? Who would find thy cure then?" She gave it a salty kiss.

Nadin was right: Adren needed help. Oh, saints in heaven, how she needed it. She only hoped she would remain sane enough to reach it in time. And now, even now that she was so sure she was calm and the nightmares would go away, a little thread remained, black as night, and it grew again in her mind until it was the sky and she was again in the place without stars.

The unicorn was there with her; she was sure of it. Its fear roared through her mind as a figure appeared out of the darkness, sword in hand. The blade rose, and Adren leapt. Her body stretched out in a bizarre configuration, feeling both impossible and familiar at the same time. Down came the sword, slicing through the air, bright, inevitable. Adren passed the figure, falling to the ground, and the pain from her forehead traced lines down her whole body, seeping into her bones.

There was a cry, and then the clash of metal as another figure fought the first, their swords meeting and falling away as if in a dance. The unicorn within the vision shrieked. Adren felt rather than saw it as it shrank back from the battle, hiding in the furthest corner it could, all while reaching to her mind in concern. She reached back, holding on to the unicorn's warmth like a lifeline, sending it strength back.

As she did, the vision began to fade, leaving behind the horrible realization.

It was a memory.

Adren reeled back, aware again of her limbs. As her vision cleared, so did her memory of the event. Only a dissipating panic remained in its place.

The unicorn stood several paces away, nostrils wide and breathing hard. Adren grimaced when she saw the scratches she had left on its neck during the episode. The feeling coming from it was a sort of paralysis. Shock.

"I'm sorry," Adren said. "I'm sorry." She stepped towards the unicorn. It flinched, then turned and ran away, leaves settling in its wake.

Great. Some kind of emotion tried to well up within her, but she pushed it down and bound it tight before it could name itself. The last thing she needed right then was more complications. Nadin himself was complication enough. While Adren was glad she wasn't alone during her episodes, there was the fact that she still didn't know how human he was. A part-fairy with occasional human ridiculousness from growing up with them, she could deal with. But a full human, despite his ability to see and do a little magic? It would be only a matter of time before he revealed his true self and turned on her.

Never trust a human. They could only pretend to be good for so long.

Oh, gods. Nadin was going to take forever at the market, wasn't he?

Nadin took a deep breath once he entered the market and let all the tension in his muscles melt away. He ambled between the stalls, pausing to inspect the fresh fruit, vegetables, and other foods brought in from farms and back gardens. All his life had been spent in towns, among the people and the bustle and, while the countryside was undeniably peaceful, he never joined in when Adren got vocal about its superiority.

The people at the stalls were friendly, and he entered into happy conversation with nearly all of them, listening to their gossip about the town or surrounding rural areas. Until they mentioned the war.

"Well, it ain't coming yet, but it will," said a farmer as he arranged the eggs in a more geometric pattern.

"It may as well already be happening," said the woman at the stall as she slapped the farmer's hand away and rearranged the eggs according to colour and size.

"There's a war?" asked Nadin, his attention drawn away from the eggs in a moment.

"Where did you say you were from again?" asked the woman.

"Watorej. But I've been travelling the past three weeks."

"That would explain it," she said. "They only just announced the draft two weeks ago."

"One and a half," said the farmer. He was eyeing the apples.

"Don't you even dare." The woman stuck her index finger in the farmer's face. "You touch them, you buy them. And it was definitely two weeks."

"The posts appeared one and a half weeks ago, but they're dated at two weeks," said the farmer, making a face.

"I'm confused. Why would they have a draft if there wasn't a war yet?" Nadin waited as a battle of wills passed over the apples, with intermittent hand-sparring.

"So that it doesn't look like we're going to have a war," said the woman after she had subdued the farmer. He sulked.

"If you would just let me organize them, it would look more attractive. You'd have more customers."

"I have enough customers. You should go attend to your own. I'm sure your wife would appreciate the help, if your organization skills are so very attractive." The woman shooed him away. "Unless you'd rather talk about the war."

"No, I'd rather talk about your people skills. Here I am, offering perfectly good help, and you turn me away. It's because you married first, isn't it?" He cut the last word short and grimaced as he watched the woman for her reaction.

She only shook her head. "I swear, Izek, if you weren't my brother and those weren't my eggs, I would climb right over this stall and force you out."

"Should I leave?" asked Nadin, stepping back.

"Not if you don't have anything important to do," said the woman. "It's a slow day. We're just bantering. There's been nothing official about the war but what with the draft and more soldiers running around everywhere, especially close to the border, they're expecting war to be declared, or they're expecting to be the ones who declare it. That is, if the rumours are true." She grinned.

"Which border?" asked Nadin.

"Breim," said the farmer, one hand inching towards the eggs. His sister slapped him again.

Nadin made a curious sound, rather like he was being strangled. The siblings gave him a curious look. He cleared his throat.

"Thank you for the news. I... I have to go." Which he did, immediately, and before anyone had a chance to say anything else. He raced through the market, face pale and drawn, ignoring the complaints of those he bumped into. As he left the market, his pace slowed, though not by much, and he looked up side streets and alleyways until he came across one that was empty. Puffs of dust rose as he entered and found a spot that wasn't visible from the street and sat down against a wall, his pack beside him. He covered his face, ran his fingers through his hair, rocked a bit in place. Took a deep breath.

"Everything all right?"

Nadin started. A young woman stood in front of him, wrapped in a yellow shawl and wearing a curious, broad-brimmed hat. Behind her jangled a cart, like a small market stall, full of a variety of objects made of glass, metal, and wood, all in forms at once both familiar and foreign.

"Please leave me alone," said Nadin, burying his face in his arms. "I really don't want to talk with anyone right now."

"Of course not. That's why you're alone in an alley. I only

thought..." She tilted her head to one side, and her voice became very soft. "Th'art part fae, art thou not?"

"What?" he lifted his head, hands clutching at his upper arms in an unconscious motion. "What did you say?"

"You've fairy blood. Not all, but enough."

They stared at each other. Nadin squinted.

"And... you're full fairy," he said with amazement.

"Aye." The fairy smiled and curtsied. Nadin nodded in return, his Adam's apple bobbing. "Well met, friend. Now, do you still wish me to leave, or is there anything I may help with?"

"No, there's nothing."

"Ah, well then. As you like." She picked back up the cart and started away through the alley, back the way Nadin had come. He stared after her, knuckles white.

"Wait."

"Aye?"

Picking up his pack, Nadin stood and walked to the fairy, dust rising and falling with every step.

"Do you have anything"—he gestured at the items on the cart—"that would cure insanity? One that might be caused by magic?"

The fairy's eyes narrowed and she tapped her chin. "That depends on the kind of insanity. To which do you refer?"

"There are... kinds?" He blinked.

"Does the afflicted see things that aren't there? Or hear them, perhaps? Have they convinced themselves of some grand unreality? Are they unusually violent? Unusually withdrawn?"

"I guess they... they can't speak. Or understand when people talk to them. They, um, run off and get into danger? They get hurt when they run off, anyhow, and they get scared really easy. It's hard to calm them down unless you know how. And unless they know you."

As he spoke, the fairy's hand hovered over one object after another but, when he came to the end of his description, the fairy frowned and closed her hand.

"Alas, I have no such cure," she said. Nadin's shoulders slumped. "I am sorry.

"No, no, it's fine. I didn't think you'd have it, anyway. But you do have—you can heal other things, right?"

The fairy nodded and set down her cart.

"Do you—might you...?" Nadin swallowed. "It's for a wasting disease. One that's slow. They get weaker and weaker as the years go by, and you can see the health go from their skin and hair. If they die, it's not for a long, long time and when their body has nothing left, their mind goes as well. They rave about... well, things that might not be real. They forget their relatives, and who the people closest to them are. They act like... like they're monsters instead."

"The cure for that requires something I cannot give," said the fairy, her voice sad and gentle.

"I can pay for it," Nadin said with an edge of pleading.

"You misunderstand. I cannot give it because I do not have it, and I do not even know where you might begin to look for it."

There was a shout from the end of the alley Nadin had come in. He and the fairy both looked towards it and, only a few moments later, a group of soldiers came into view, pointing at Nadin and telling him to stay where he was.

"Don't worry," said the fairy. Nadin turned to her and jerked back. To ordinary human eyes, that part of the alley would appear empty but, to the eyes of one with fairy blood, the fairy could still be seen, but as if she stood behind mist. "If you have done nothing wrong, you have nothing to fear."

Adren kept invisible as the two groups of soldiers, coming from opposite ends of the alley, converged on Nadin. He and they exchanged a few words that Adren couldn't get close enough to hear. This apparently didn't go well for Nadin. The soldiers grabbed him and escorted him out and away from the market.

What would have happened if she had come sooner to find Nadin? Bah. Knowing him, probably the exact same thing.

When they'd left her sight, Adren let go of the invisibility. She was about to come out from behind the large wooden box she'd hidden behind—just in case—when a young woman with a cart of fairy-made objects appeared in the middle of the alley. Invisibility? No. Considering her clothing and the contents of the cart, the young woman had to be a fairy, and they preferred illusion over magic of more substance. That and Adren was fairly certain fairies couldn't turn invisible the way she could.

The fairy sighed and picked up her cart. Adren stepped out from behind the box.

"Wait."

Halting, the fairy glanced over Adren and frowned.

"What art thou? I perceive thy magic, but cannot uncover its nature."

"I'm not like you," Adren said, refusing to respond with 'thee'. To do so would be tantamount to claiming to be a magical creature, and this she could not do.

"Nay, thou art. It may be piecemeal only, but thou and I do have kinship of a sort." Her brow furrowed even deeper as she leaned in a little, then relaxed as she drew back and nodded. "That aside, what wouldst thou ask of me?"

"The boy that the soldiers took away, did you speak with him before they came?"

"Aye. Knowest thou him?"

Adren wondered what they had spoken about. "He and I travel together. Do you know where they took him? And why?"

The fairy was silent for a moment as she tapped her chin with one finger.

"Aye. They thought him Breimic, and will have him in prison."

Breimic? Adren supposed Nadin did look it, though not obviously, and could easily have been born in Breim and come to live in Watorej after. But there was the problem of his name and accent, both of which were entirely Iderish. No, he couldn't be Breimic. More likely he'd said the wrong thing at the wrong time, had been misunderstood, and someone had informed the authorities.

Still, Adren felt part of herself soften towards the boy, who might be one of her countrymen.

"Dost thou plan to free him?"

"Won't they let him go? He's harmless."

"Nay, they shan't. They dare not give Breim any chance for knowledge of their plans for war."

"Ider wants to declare war on Breim? I hope all they're expecting to gain is a few chickens and maybe a canoe." They both laughed.

"Humans," remarked the fairy with a smirk. Adren grinned. Then frowned. If Nadin really was part fairy, she couldn't just leave him behind.

"Do you know how to get into the prison?"

A smile lit up the fairy's face. She gestured to the paraphernalia on her cart. "That and more. I am called Loram."

"I'm Adren."

"Come, Adren, let us meddle."

CHAPTER
TWO

"I'm not a spy!" Nadin protested for the fifth time since the soldiers had dragged him away. By this point, the soldiers just ignored him.

The market served as the town's centre, at the crossing of two main roads. Nadin had entered the town from the south, along the road he and Adren had been travelling parallel to for the past few days. The soldiers had taken him north and east along the other main road, past shops, inns, a livery barn. He and Adren had planned on staying in an inn that night, but all talk of that had ended the moment her fit began.

Now they turned off the main road, following a tree-lined side street until they came to a large walled building at the edge of town, a sign with the word "Prison" on it helpfully placed above the main door.

The air around the prison shivered with magic, but not the fairy kind. The soldiers walked through it without trouble, but Nadin slowed at its boundary. The magic shuddered as he entered, bright lines of it like veins shooting from the place where he went through.

"Come on!" said one of the soldiers. "Slowing down isn't going to get you out of this." They grabbed him and pulled. Nadin stared up at the magic, eyes wide and eyebrows raised so high they caused his forehead to wrinkle.

The shape of the magic froze, the lines undulating in place. Then they stopped and, quick as a bubble popping, returned to normal. If not for the soldiers, Nadin would have fallen over. As it was, they grumbled at him for losing his balance.

He gave it one last glance before they took him through the doors, but the paper-thin wall did nothing more than shimmer.

Loram's cart would be a problem. She and Adren decided the best course would be to return it to the mound and, while there, ask for help from the other fairies.

"The humans here are wise in the ways of fairies," Loram said. "And we have had some trouble of late regarding the prison. Methinks it best we do not attempt this on our own, much as I'd wish to."

And much as Adren wished to. Still, getting fairy help was worth the delay, in her opinion.

"An thou have discomfort among the fae, thou canst wait, but I would not advise such."

"Why not?" Adren raised an eyebrow. She didn't expect discomfort among fairies. Before leaving to search for a cure for the unicorn, and for as far back as she could remember, she had lived among fairies. What she had expected even less was for a fairy to advise against her staying outside the mound. Fairies tended to be choosy about who they allowed into their places. Only other fairies had any assurance of permanent access to any sites they claimed as their own. Only other fairies could expect both welcome and open invitation.

Loram shook her head. "It should not be discussed here. Shalt thou follow?"

"I will."

The fairy led Adren through the streets away from the market, taking so many turns and "shortcuts" that Adren gave up trying to keep track of their location. The cart rattled against the cobblestones, and a set of pendants at the top jangled in cacophony with the clang of the metal and glass of the rest of her wares. As soon as Adren's attention caught the sound, she couldn't let it go. It penetrated her skull and ached in her ears, but she could think of no way to escape it. Except that the one pulling in the cart was, in fact, a fairy.

"Could you...?"

"Aye?"

Adren pointed at the cart. "The noise."

With a grin, Loram nodded and quiet returned. Adren smiled wide. If only Nadin could perform illusions instead of just being able to see through them. Or, if he did have that ability, enough knowledge and confidence to make the magic work. It would certainly be an improvement from his unreliable ability to see magic.

If she was honest with herself, Adren wanted Nadin to be

nothing more than a misguided human. Inferior. He could remain clumsy, naive, incompetent... but that was the thing. He wasn't incompetent. In Watorej, it was he who had come up with the plan to break into the lord's mansion, he who had located the sealskin, he who had kept going when she could not. If she could have dismissed him as a human, then everything would be simple. But she couldn't. She couldn't, and it bothered her.

Her agitation filtered through the connection at the back of her mind, and she felt the unicorn's emotions shift in response. It hadn't been happy with her leaving it when she'd gone to find Nadin and, instead of going off and minding itself, as usual, it had kept close to the forest all this time, sending her bursts of anxiety with every slight change of her mood. Adren had never known the unicorn to behave in this exact way, but it wasn't so out of character that it troubled her. Even now, its response to her was mild compared to its usual, enough that she didn't need to calm herself to keep it peaceful. She did so, anyway, out of habit.

The unicorn could have healed the scratches Adren had left on Nadin's arms easily but Nadin, still unused to this, had likely forgotten, and Adren hadn't wanted him to stay. She could have let it come right away and heal him and then sent him off to the town after; she'd had enough control over that episode to keep it at bay that long. And yet, the thought hadn't even crossed her mind. Did that mean something?

"Thou art very quiet," observed Loram.

"I don't like conversation."

"Ah."

They continued in silence for a bit, passing out of the town and into trees, deeper and deeper into the leaf-filtered light. The road they followed seemed to appear out of nothing before them a bit at a time, and to disappear behind them in the same fashion. Adren knew this sort of fairy magic well—both an aid to friendly travel and protection for the mound against intruders.

"Thy friend, before his arrest, asked of me a cure for a kind of madness." Adren held her breath a moment and her step faltered, but Loram continued as if she hadn't noticed. "What he then described was strange, an insanity I have never before heard of, and I had no choice but to say that I could not aid him. I have thought longer on this and... it is obvious he spoke not of thee, but I wonder: Doth he search for this cure himself, or is that thy mission and he only asked on thy behalf?"

"He asked for me." No doubt after asking for treatment for his own injuries and a cure for his mother, but still. He did ask.

"I thought as much. His description was, well, clinical. And yet, it has remained in my thoughts to the point where I understand I might have been hasty in my answer to him. Alone, I may do nothing for this madness, but I need not act alone. With the others in the mound, methinks I can effect this cure for you."

Adren's heart fell. "I wish you could. I've already asked fairies for help. It didn't work."

"They must have little to impress if they could not do even that." In the canopy, a chickadee sang its name as they passed, the dees nearly unending.

"They are the kindest people I know," said Adren quietly. Loram shrugged.

"It remains that we may do for thee what they could not. Thou mayest doubt this, but I assure thee that my words are truth." One of the cart's wheels got stuck on a rock. "Bah, I always forget this spot." A faint touch of honeysuckle spread over Adren's tongue as her truth sense flared. At forgetting? But not Loram's statement about the fairies helping with a cure. Odd.

As they worked to free the cart, Adren reminded herself there wasn't anything to worry about. Just because someone didn't deeply believe a statement to be true didn't mean they were lying. Loram wasn't human and, as such, could be trusted. It could mean that Loram had doubts—and rightfully so, since all she had was a description of the unicorn's madness. It could mean nothing.

And yet.

Nadin had been different than she'd expected.

No, no, no! There could be no middle ground. Either Nadin was human and therefore not to be trusted, or he wasn't.

Cart freed, they set off again, and exhaustion fell over Adren, inevitable as snow in winter. The unicorn might come to her then, come through and interrupt, but Adren didn't care. They were in the forest, away from humans. Let it come. It didn't; it kept its distance, instead sending strength and warmth. One day, she would see it healed. One day...

"I hope thou hast finished thy thoughts. We arrive."

The path before them had opened up to reveal a large, smooth mound in which was set a low threshold of stone. Trees grew around it, but they left it bare and stood back from its doorway, as if aware of the needs of its residents.

"You're sure I'm allowed in?"

"An th'art accompanied by one of us, thou mayest enter. And thou mayest stay as long as thou keepest with me. Which thou wilt do?" Loram gave Adren an anxious look.

"Of course."

Loram went in first, back straight, and the threshold grew to fit her and her cart. As she followed, Adren let her gaze linger on the stone, expecting to see decoration, only to find it rough and bare. It could have been illusion, or it could be that these fairies didn't care much for art in their doorway. Too bad. The art on the threshold where she came from had always been her favourite, all the carvings of strange beasts and human-like figures, the intricate patterns of writing she had never learned to read twisting among them. Their flowing forms had always fascinated her, their shapes so different from the angular human writing. She had often wondered what it said, but the fairies had never taught her to read it and had never read it to her, no matter how much she asked.

The stone slabs gave way to a dirt tunnel. Illusion most certainly, especially since it ended only a few paces in and neither turned nor had any branches. Adren stopped when Loram did.

"Shalt thou not continue onwards?"

"Is it the entrance?"

"Whyever wouldn't it be?" A smile tugged at the corners of Loram's mouth.

Adren raised an eyebrow. "Because it's too obvious."

Loram laughed, throwing her head back and putting her hands to her stomach. Adren smiled, but didn't quite understand the joke.

"Oh," said Loram, wiping her eyes, "oh, truly th'art not like to humankind. But why wouldst thou not admit it?"

"It's complicated," said Adren. "Where's the entrance?"

Loram stepped back a couple paces and pointed to the wall on her left. She then walked into and through it, pulling the cart behind her, looking for all the world as if she passed through a cleverly hidden opening. When Adren followed, it became clear that this was not the case. At the edge of the illusion, she could feel dirt, could watch as bits of it fell away as she pushed through the crust of feeling and beyond to the true fairy tunnels.

Nadin shifted on the cot again and grimaced. Sighing, he got up and sat on the floor of the prison cell instead. He tapped on his knees, drumming a simple rhythm, his gaze travelling along the walls, the ceiling. Not the door with its barred window. Definitely the pile of... something... in the corner. Nadin wrinkled his nose at that, whatever it was, and resumed his survey.

"Very soon, Adren will come," he sang softly, a tuneless melody in time with his drumming. "Because I can't figure out a way to get out. And no-one here will see reason and let me go. They think I'm a spy, which is ridiculous; I'm terrible at staying quiet. I'm terrible at not getting caught. I'm terrible at sneaking. I'm terrible at..." He sighed, stood, brushed at his pants. Said: "I'm just terrible at everything."

The pile of things in the corner of the cell proved too ambiguous to ignore. Nadin went over to it, still tapping away on his legs, and leaned in for closer inspection. With only a thumb and forefinger, he picked up a rag, and a very soiled one at that. Aside from a bright spot of red that he had uncovered, the entire pile was nothing more than a collection of dirty bits of cloth. Sighing and dropping the rag, Nadin sat back against the wall next to the pile. Then he looked back at it, at the bit of red. He shrugged and started tossing rags to the side, staring at the thing that was taking shape beneath them, nose so wrinkled that his expression was a little unnatural.

Bit by bit, the rags fell away, revealing brown amidst the red, and a shape that anyone would recognize at once in a different context. In this context, it took until the thing was wholly uncovered before it was seen for what it was: A hand. But just a hand.

Nadin cried out and fell back.

"Finally found it, did you?" said one of the guards not far from the cell. The other laughed.

"Why the hell is there a severed hand in here?" yelled Nadin, eyes wide, frozen in a half-fallen, half-crouching position.

"Oh, I'm sure you can think of something." By now, both of them were sniggering.

"But it's rotting! Do you have any idea how unsanitary this is?"

The guards' laughter only increased in volume.

"Aren't you going to do anything about it?"

There was a pause, at which Nadin perked up... followed by more mirth. He slumped and sat on the floor. Glanced at the hand. Scooted away from it.

Glanced at it again.

The cell smelled of stone and sweat, of musty bedsheets and dry air. Nadin sniffed. He leaned towards the hand and sniffed some more. His expression changed to confusion as he approached the hand a little bit at a time, testing the air as he went. Finally, he came close enough to touch it. With a trembling finger, Nadin reached out until he came in contact with the hand's hard surface, at which point his eyebrows lifted so fast that they nearly took off and flew up to the ceiling. He grabbed one of the fingers, cringing as he did, and pulled at it.

It didn't budge.

Because the hand was made of wood.

At that moment, the laughter stopped. It didn't die out; it just stopped, immediately and all at once, as if chopped through with a knife. Nadin stood and turned to face the door. Nothing more enlightening than silence came through it, but Nadin didn't move right away. He waited, ear turned towards the door, and frowned.

"Why is there magic out there?"

CHAPTER
THREE

The roots of trees carved out the air between them as if the space of the tunnels were the intrusion, not the dirt around them. They knobbled their way down and around walls, ceilings, and entrances, with small threadlike rootlets hanging down to brush against the top of the cart and, in some cases, Loram's head when she didn't duck. After they put the cart away and went deeper into the mound, they came to passageways where the rootlets had been trimmed or tucked out of the way. It was a minor act of domestication that did nothing to tame the trees' foundations.

"Where is everyone?" Adren asked.

"Out, it would seem," Loram replied with a huff. And then, muttering, "They could have told me they planned to—"

Laughter rang through the mound, and with it the pounding of voices and the acid tang of magic against the skin. Adren rubbed her cheek where one spark had stung her quite badly. Back home, they'd kept that part of their jubilation in check around her, at least. She'd forgotten how annoying it was.

Three fairies rounded the bend, hooting. They stopped when they saw Adren, their carefree expressions turned tense with distrust.

"What bringst thou here?" asked the one on the right. She was slim and graceful, with hair to her waist, enough that she could have pretended to be a tree spirit and led humans on a merry chase through the woods if she wanted. Adren thought she probably did, and often. The fairy had her arm around the waist of the tallest of them, a handsome fairy with brown hair only a shade darker than his skin.

Loram stiffened. "A friend, and none other. I wish to speak with the monarchs on her behalf—would you three keep her company while I do?"

The monarchs? Adren hadn't realized Loram would go to them for help. Was the prison really so well guarded?

"Thou hast been low on luck of late," the spirit-like fairy commented. Her intonation held an undercurrent that was far from harmless.

"Aye, and this one may change it. Wait with her?"

The three fairies regarded Adren with interest. Oh, saints.

"Don't think of playing tricks on me," Adren said. "I grew up with fairies. I know how you think."

"Is that so?" The spirit-like one gave a sly smile.

"I, at least, shall wait for thee, Loram," said the tall one with a laugh. "Methinks your friend shall provide excellent entertainment." Loram nodded, but turned to the spirit-like one for her answer. Adren wondered at the hierarchy between the three. Clearly, both Loram and the man had lower positions than the woman, but exactly how high *was* her position?

"And I as well," said the spirit-like fairy. "Go off on thy business, Loram. Thy friend is welcome."

Loram nodded and sped off down the tunnel.

"Well..." The spirit-like one put a finger to her chin. "Thou'rt not fae."

Adren winced. "Please, call me not thou."

"Thou'rt not human, either," said the third fairy, a boy of around Nadin's age with a Breimic accent. Not older, Adren thought, but no more than two years younger. It must be his first time visiting another mound.

"Anyone can see that," the tall one said, chuckling. Heat rose in Adren's face.

"I am Adren, and only myself. Please," she spoke more firmly this time, "call me not thou."

"Adren who is neither fae nor human, my name is Barsae." The tall fairy gave a shallow bow.

"And I am Iraem," said the spirit-like one. There was a pause, and they both looked pointedly at the boy, who had been scowling since Barsae's comment about Adren.

"What?"

"Introduce thyself, boy. We have a guest. Don't be rude." Barsae gave a significant glance in Adren's direction.

"Oh. I... er... I'm Hinor. Call me Hin." The scowl vanished, replaced with such an air of awkwardness, Adren could have sworn Nadin had escaped prison by himself and entered the fairy mound in disguise.

"But are you truly no magical being?" asked Iraem. "Your appearance is so unlike humans."

"Why can she be rude and I can't?" Hin asked Barsae.

Adren laughed. She'd missed fairies. Oh, saints, how she'd missed fairies.

"Because she's an adult," Adren said. "Adults may pick their rules and find an they like what results."

Iraem and Barsae nodded, beaming. Hin sulked.

"Truly, you *have* lived with fairies," remarked Iraem.

"Do you return from a revel? Loram seemed unhappy to be left out."

"Of sorts," said Barsae, grinning. Iraem frowned at him, but didn't say anything. She didn't have time. Loram stalked in, expression sour, and there was an odd flurry of looks between the fairies that Adren was too surprised to follow.

"Come," Loram told Adren. "We will find no help here." She grabbed Adren by the arm and left the others without another word. Adren turned back for a farewell, but only had the time to catch a glance of Iraem, arm slung over Barsae's shoulder, whispering something to him that made his smile want to reach his ears. He nodded to her and they went off, Hin trotting along behind. Before they turned the corner, Iraem's shawl slipped. As she fixed it, Adren caught sight of ridged skin on her back. Was it…? But the shawl was back in place before Adren could be sure.

They left the mound faster than they had come, and this entirely due to the speed at which Loram pulled Adren along. The tunnels had traffic through them now, but Loram wove through it without hesitation. Some of the fairies they passed communicated their surprise, the majority of which was directed at Adren's presence rather than Loram's rudeness.

When they had arrived back in the forest, Adren wrenched herself free of Loram's grasp. This wasn't hard, as Loram had loosened her grip and slowed her pace now that they were above the surface.

"I take it the monarchs liked not what you had to say." Adren spoke sharply, annoyed at how Loram had treated her. She rubbed at the soreness of the place where Loram had grabbed her arm.

"The monarchs like not me, is more to the point," Loram replied, her back to Adren.

"Does that stop us from what we intend?"

Loram sighed. "No. But it would have helped."

A call rang out from behind. Adren turned to see Hin running towards them.

"Loram! The monarchs have reconsidered. They wish to speak with her."

Nadin peered through the bars.

"Well, it's definitely not Adren," he commented, eyes following the trails of magic. They weren't in the prison, but rather somewhere outside it. Like the wall that had slowed Nadin down, their flashing was visible only to those with Nadin's ability. "Anyone want to guess the odds those fairies are coming to rescue me?" He snorted.

The magic, though explosive when it had first appeared, had died down by this point. Only a few faint threads had made their way past the prison's magic, and these faded without doing anything of consequence. One made its way into his cell and left a pink streak on the floor. Nadin shrugged and sat on the cot again. He drummed on his knees.

"Hey, you awake there?" said one of the guards. Nadin was about to answer when the other guard replied, "I have about had it with these saintsall fairies. We sent her back, didn't we? Why can't they just leave us in peace?"

"That bad this time, huh?"

"I'd like to punch whoever thought it was a good idea to hire someone to cast a barrier that didn't keep their spells from knocking everyone unconscious every time they decide to pay a visit. Denyeh's fees aren't unreasonable." Nadin, who had not been knocked unconscious, frowned and inclined his head towards the door.

"Talk to the captain about it."

"He said he couldn't 'justify the expense'."

"I swear he was dropped on his head when he was a baby. Our old captain had sense."

"Poor Denyeh."

"Yeah." The first guard sighed. "I guess this was the best they could do on short notice."

The other guard grunted his assent. "Still, would have been nice if she'd been telling the truth about having the Saint's Gauntlet. If that thing even exists, I'd love to use it to go give those fairies a piece of my mind."

"I'd give them more than that."

"What's the Saint's Gauntlet?" asked Nadin.

"Shut up," growled the guard. When the two began talking again, it had nothing to do with armour of any kind.

Like the tunnels of the fairy mound, roots lined the walls of the throne room. Some also spread across the floor, forming both dais and thrones, upon which sat the monarchs wearing long green robes and crowned with oak leaves. To the king's left, in a smaller throne and similarly dressed, sat Iraem.

Ah. *That* high.

Loram had been stopped at the door, but another fairy had brought Adren to the edge of the dais, where the monarchs and Iraem appraised her.

"We hear you have need of our aid," said the queen.

"Aye. I seek a cure for madness, after I have freed my..." Friend? Colleague? No, definitely not. "Working partner from prison."

"What have you to offer in exchange for these favours?"

"What wish you to have?"

The monarchs leaned back, and the queen steepled her fingers. Adren hadn't meant her question as an open offer— rather, it had been to establish the need they wanted filled. Among the fairies she knew, this would be understood, but these fairies seemed to have understood it the first way. She stopped herself just in time from biting her lip. No need to let them know what she was thinking.

"We are concerned," the king pronounced, "that aiding you would mean we have allied ourselves with one whose character is suspect. What would you say of our thought that you are the White Changeling?"

Why would they care? Fairies didn't involve themselves in human affairs, nor cared about human conceptions of morality. It was humans who had decided Adren was the White Changeling and what that meant. But these were fairy monarchs asking, and it wouldn't do to be cantankerous with them.

"I would say you are correct, although I'm not a changeling."

The king waved his hand. "No matter. Humans know little of the ways of fairies; we had no opinion either way on the accuracy of the name. What we seek to validate is the accuracy of your reputation."

Adren couldn't help but wonder which part of her reputation he referred to. Did their information come from before or after—?

"Do you regularly commit thievery and violence upon humans, no matter their stature?" asked the queen.

"Yes." After, then.

"Would you do those things at our request?"

"To humans?"

"To humans."

"Yes." They were only humans, after all.

The queen gestured to a fairy at the back, who opened the door to let Loram in and accompanied her to the dais.

"We shall give aid in this way," the king proclaimed. "Loram may work with you. Go to the prison and do what you need, take what you need, and we shall give what we may of what you wish when you return. Be warned: the humans have placed over the prison a barrier which fairies and any of our magic able to take it down cannot cross so, Adren, know that you will have to find some way to undo it before Loram may enter the prison."

"That is no aid," Loram muttered.

On the contrary, Adren thought that the information about the barrier was useful, as well as an explanation for why all they could do was send one fairy with her.

"And in return?" Adren asked, head high.

"This working partner of yours," said the queen. "We would like him."

Adren's heart thudded. "You want... Nadin?"

"Aye."

The throne room seemed to have gotten smaller around Adren. Give Nadin to them? The fairies she'd lived with hadn't condoned kidnapping, but she knew other fairies liked to take humans and use them as entertainment or workers. Did that mean he was human? But if he was human, then she had no need to worry. Let them have him; it would be safer for her that way. Unless he wasn't human.

No, no, this was silly! Loram had seen Nadin. She knew what he was, and she must have told the monarchs. Which meant that, if he wasn't human, then they wouldn't use him. They would treat him as their own. Maybe even help his mother, if they were in the mood. If they could. Magical creatures wouldn't harm one of their own.

If he was a human, well. He would get what he deserved, and Adren would finally see the unicorn cured.

After all those years of searching, the unicorn's suffering

would be over. She could see it already, restored to its senses, in full possession and control of its magic. The journey could find its end at last. Adren and the unicorn both would have peace. Adren wouldn't have been able to hide her grin even if she wanted to. In the back of her mind, the unicorn's anxiety ebbed, replaced by a swelling excitement.

"I accept."

At this, the queen smiled. "We thought you might. Loram?"

"Aye, I accept." She didn't look happy about it.

FOUR

"What if I never get out of here?" Nadin asked the wooden hand. "That's not just me being dramatic, is it? You would think Adren would have come by now, at least to see what the fairies were up to. Do you think she'd ask fairies for help? Do you think they'd offer any?" He shivered. Straightened. "Why am I talking to a wooden hand, anyways? Come on Nadin, get it together. You haven't been in here long. No need to worry yet."

The wooden hand had nothing to offer in consolation. Neither did the guards, for that matter. They had returned to their table outside his cell and were now engrossed in a game of cards. While the game wasn't visible from Nadin's barred window, one who was familiar with its rules would recognize from their talk that they were playing yuker and that they were both probably cheating.

"I know exactly what Adren will say when she finds me here. 'You just had to talk to people, didn't you? I would never get in this situation. I don't talk to people.

People are stupid.'" Nadin stuck out his tongue. "Well, what if I say I can't help it; I like people? And I was curious." He then frowned in put-on grumpiness. "'Oh, fine, be curious. But be smart about it, like me. Don't be like people. I'm not people, and look at how I turned out.'" With a sigh, he lay back on the cot. "Case in point."

Loram kept the two of them unseen and unheard while Adren took stock of the prison. Outer wooden walls surrounded a small yard, with ugly inner stone walls to wrap the squat building. The sloped roof ended in a large overhang, enough that Adren could tell she wouldn't be able to climb down from it into any windows. Of course, this being a prison, none of the windows would open.

Guards stood at every possible entrance, all armed, all appearing more or less competent. Using invisibility to get past them might work, but she wouldn't be able to hold it much longer by the time she got inside. Excellent. A challenge.

"Where's the barrier?" Adren asked.

"It lies a handspan away from the walls and the same above the highest point of the roof. A cheap design, as it would let through the effects of any fairy magic it blocked, but effective. I cannot see any break in it."

It may have been more than Adren had asked, but all useful information. Nadin could learn a thing or two from Loram. Perhaps he would.

"Do you see how it might be taken down?"

"From the inside of the prison itself. 'Twould be simple

enough for me if I could enter, but I see not how such a feat could be achieved. If I told you the shape of it, would you…?"

Adren hesitated. She hadn't done much with her magic since it had revealed itself, in the hopes that it would die down or go away entirely. And while she hadn't lost control since Watorej, she still found it difficult to make it do what she wanted.

"I don't know. How complicated is it?"

"It isn't." Loram paused. "Except you cannot see it, so then it might be for you."

"Could you make it visible? Or enough of it visible so I could tear it down?"

Loram rubbed underneath her chin and stared off into the distance. Adren walked a few steps away to get a different angle of the prison. Perhaps she *could* use her invisibility, if she had to go all the way inside regardless. That would rely on more than a little luck that she could find a convenient hiding place near the entrance so she could rest a moment before becoming invisible again. But how long would it take to find Nadin? And unlock his door. And get him out and away. Small inanimate objects that fit in her pockets were one thing, but keeping herself and another person invisible took more to sustain and didn't last as long as a result. If she wasn't sure about getting herself in, she liked the chances of getting him out even less.

"Adren!" exclaimed Loram, laughing.

"What?"

"I have a marvelous idea." She gave a quick outline, involving both an illusion for distraction and a small spell to guide Adren to the right place. Adren couldn't help but grin. Until she thought of the key task she would have to perform.

"Even if all that worked and I arrived where the enchantment was, are you certain I would be able to end it? A child of your kind could work their magic better than I can work mine."

"Working magic isn't so difficult as you make it seem."

"I assure you, it is."

"No it isn't. Watch." Loram stepped back and a glowing form unlike anything Adren had ever seen appeared in the air between them. It looked something like a cloud, if a cloud also had rivers. "This is how the enchantment in the prison appears to mine eyes. Cast a stripe of magic of sufficient strength here"—the spot turned blue—"and the enchantment will crumble. Like so." A line appeared along the blue part as if drawn by an invisible brush, and the form unravelled. After a pause, it reformed itself, complete with the blue patch. "Your turn."

Loram didn't understand. How could she, after playing with magic her whole life? Adren had watched fairy children practise and study the use of magic for years to be able to make full use of their abilities, and they played for years before that to develop the kind of coordination Loram had just displayed. If Adren couldn't even make light when she wanted, a line was most certainly out of the question. She shook her head.

"Oh, saints, you're one of *those*," complained Loram.

"One of what?"

With a grin, Loram tapped her forehead. "Over-thinkers.

Someone told you magic was complicated, and now you seek only ways in which to make it difficult for yourself."

Adren tried to give a retort, but no sound came out. Loram's grin got bigger. She pointed at the spell-form.

"You may wish to know I have a deft hand with curses."

Since Adren could still feel her vocal chords working, she knew her muteness was only an illusion at the moment but, gods in hell, Adren could tell Loram meant it about the curses.

Adren's magic flowed beneath her skin, an ever-shifting movement of potential. Of possibility. She reached out, index finger on blue light, and let some of her magic trickle through as she drew her hand across to trace the line Loram had made.

Nothing happened. The magic stayed at her fingertip. She frowned at it, as if that alone would get it to do what she wanted. Not that she expected it to comply but, gods, life would be so much easier if it *would*.

"Loosen your hold some," Loram advised. "Let it move more freely, and let more of it move."

Like when she'd let it explode and burn the people who'd tried to hurt her? No, there was a vast difference between the two scenarios. The magic no longer cried out that she use it, no longer pressed itself against her control, ready to break free into a flood. She had exploded and they'd settled into a truce. Still, it wasn't one she wanted to jeopardize.

Oh, this was silly. Here she was with someone who knew how to use magic and who, unlike Nadin, had confidence in her use of it. If Adren needed to break this enchantment, she now found herself in the ideal circumstances to learn how. Might as well make use of them.

This time, when Adren lifted her hand, she didn't hold so tightly to the magic. It waited at her fingertip, swirling in readiness to act at her direction. By increments, she released more of it until her whole hand could feel it dance along her skin, fire without the burning. As she brought it in contact with the blue, she let it stick, let it stay suspended in the air while she swept her arm down and bid it to unbind, to break, to...

Another hand swept down, another hand and another magic. No, not another magic. A sword.

This was wrong, all wrong. Her own magic sparked, catalyzed in a blaze. She cut off the flow at once, but the sword was still on its path towards her, like it always was.

Next Adren knew, she was on the ground and her forehead throbbed with fading pain. She would have been worried about what happened right after doing the magic and right before opening her eyes if it weren't for the fact that most of it had faded from memory. Even the unicorn gave her no hint of how severe the attack had been. Loram stood over her, hands on her hips and eyebrows raised.

"Could you do that again, without unconsciousness after? You would be sure to end the enchantment in such a manner."

"That would work?" Adren had thought she would have to be as precise as Loram had.

"Aye, it would. And magnificently. Know you not how stopping magic works?" Loram held out a hand and helped

Adren to her feet.

"Your magic must interfere with its purpose, and be strong enough to overpower it."

"And how do you use the least magic to that end?"

The least magic? Adren knew how magic worked, but not how to use it efficiently. She hadn't considered there was a strategy to that.

"Are we still hidden in your illusion?"

"Not for lack of trying on your magic's part. What you released attempted to break the illusion, and it took quite the dance to keep it from doing so. But do not think I will let you avoid my question so easily."

"I don't know."

"Have you had no one to teach you? I learned this as a child! What of those fairies you claim to have lived with?"

It would be a little hard to teach someone how to use magic when you don't know they have it and they can't access it. Just a little. That said, it wasn't necessary for Adren to get into her whole history.

"There was no opportunity for it."

"So, you've used your magic so little you can hardly direct it, and you've never been told how you might use it to your advantage, am I correct?"

"Yes." Put like that, Adren sounded like a dunce. Which she probably was, from Loram's perspective. All this time among humans and their ignorance of much to do with magic, having none of their own, had made Adren arrogant. Yet another reason why she needed to return home. The fairies there would smack sense back into her, just as Loram was now.

"Well, there's not time for a lesson now. Mayhap after our prison break, at which point I shall have to lecture you about things I found dull as a child, but which you shall find useful now. Until then, can you do with your magic what you did just now? Without falling over?"

"I could try."

So she did. Several times, most without resulting in an attack—although many that almost undid Loram's illusion again—and with Loram giving pointers each time for how to keep from losing control and setting on fire everything around her in the prison that would burn. Which was certainly useful.

"What if Adren's taking this long because she's run into trouble?" Nadin sat bolt upright. "What if she doesn't know I'm here? What if she can't get through the barrier? Oh, hell, what if *she's* in danger and needs *my* help?" He jumped off the cot, a much more vigorous action than necessary considering how low to the ground it was. "What if she's had one of those attacks again and she's stuck out there in the forest waiting for me? After all, she said she'd wait, and..." He made a face. "Oh, who am I kidding? Adren wouldn't wait that long. Which is worse, because she could be in the middle of town, and the unicorn could come for her, which means someone would see it, and then they'd try to get it and it wouldn't be able to do anything for Adren and all I'd be doing is talking to myself about how horrible prison is."

"Are you ever going to shut up?" one of the guards yelled

in at him. "Your muttering is driving me crazy."

Nadin did shut up for a while. Until his eyes widened.

"Has she ever had an attack that ended on its own?" He paled. Magic danced at the edge of his fingertips, but he shook his head. "I can't."

On the other side of the door, one of the guards had discovered the other had been hiding extra cards. The argument that ensued revealed that both had indeed been cheating, and ended in an agreement to play the game right. For the sake of honour.

By the end of it, Nadin sat with his head in his hands.

"I'm sorry, Adren."

Inside the prison, Adren followed the faint streak of light as it sped along the corridors. Loram had enacted a tiny spell, a harmless enough spell that the barrier would let it through. Illusion wouldn't count, so the light was real light, and it had to move like real light and look like real light, as well as be faint enough that none of the guards would take any special notice of it. Adren marvelled at how Loram could do something so precise so easily.

Of course, Adren held on to her invisibility while following it, but only as a precaution. Loram had created an illusion outside the barrier of all the fairies attacking at once, plus a dragon. A tiny one, because Loram was one fairy and it was already a large illusion, but a dragon nonetheless. It really was too bad Adren couldn't spare a glance to see it herself, so she'd had to content herself with the stupefied expression of one of the guards as she stole his keys.

He'd had a lot of keys. Adren hoped it wouldn't take her too long to find the right one before unlocking Nadin's door.

The streak of light entered the captain's office. As soon as Adren closed the door and let go of her invisibility, the light sped up a stack of papers leaning against the wall and then out to a spot a couple of handspans away. It bloomed around the enchantment before disappearing to leave behind an even fainter trace of blue just above Adren's eye level. She took a breath. Let it out.

You can do this, Adren.

As she let the magic begin to flow around her fingers, her throat tightened and anxiety passed through the connection to the unicorn. It responded in kind, at greater intensity. Saints. Not now. Calm, she had to be calm.

Adren kept her breath slow and even as she put her hand on the blue trace and let her magic flow out and dismantle the enchantment. Hopefully. Not being able to see magic made this all a little more difficult than it really should have been. How did humans do it? For that matter, how did anyone other than fairies do it?

The unicorn, unconvinced by her tenuous calm, sent back spurts of greater and greater worry. Adren wanted to stop, but she couldn't. When the blue trace was gone, the enchantment would be, too, and stopping meant starting all over again, meant Loram wouldn't be able to hold her illusion long enough and the guards would come back.

Hold on, Adren, hold on.

The unicorn started moving towards Adren. It wouldn't be nearby anytime soon, which helped, but there was half a town it would have to get through first, which didn't. She tried to steady herself, and almost had it when she slipped on the magic and a streak of it shot through her like lightning—and her heart would not stop pounding. A memory rose from the dark place in her mind as it did, and she fumbled to stop it before it left her body to wreak havoc.

"You can do this, Adren. Hold on. Hold on."

She couldn't tell where the voice came from. It floated around the memory's picture as if it wanted to belong, as if it might have belonged.

A little girl with a unicorn. The girl frowned, leaned forward, then something happened and she laughed. Behind them, a man dressed in black sat by a fire and smiled. He looked familiar, but Adren couldn't place him. This bothered her even as the memory faded and the only pieces her magic could catch and hold were the girl and the fire. And the peace. Because there had been peace when the girl laughed. Peace and release.

In the air of the prison room, the blue trace disappeared. Beyond the town, the unicorn left off its approach.

Adren stopped the flow of her magic to the sound of a dragon roaring. A small roar for a dragon, but a roar nonetheless. She grinned, made herself invisible, and left the room.

The roar shook Nadin's cell. He perked up and went to look out the window. Of course, at that moment, there was no one outside the window. Some time before, another guard had run in, talking about some kind of attack.

The cards had been summarily abandoned.

Outside the prison, fairy magic flashed, no longer impeded by the barrier. The window didn't give a good angle for viewing what this magic did, but Nadin stayed at it, craning his neck this way and that and squinting. He was so preoccupied that he almost didn't turn around at the jangle of keys at his cell door.

Almost.

But not quite.

"Adren?" Nadin peeked out at her from between the bars of his cell.

Who *else* would it be? She waved at him to be quiet and kept trying keys. Didn't fit... didn't fit... didn't fit... her chest ached... didn't fit...

"I won't be able to keep them convinced for much longer." Loram came into sight and waved at Nadin. His mouth dropped open.

"What's going on?" Nadin asked.

"Shopping," Adren snapped.

"For you!" Loram giggled. Both Adren and Nadin raised an eyebrow at her. She crossed her arms. "Oh, I see. I'm not allowed to be funny."

"That wasn't funny," Adren remarked, turning back to the keys. How about this one? It slid into the lock and, when she turned it, the lock opened with a click. Using her lock-picking tools would have been faster than this. Next time something like this happened, she'd have to remember them. Rescuing Nadin would be so much easier with them handy.

Except she wouldn't have to rescue him anymore.

Ignoring the odd twist in her stomach, Adren opened the door and checked to make sure none of the guards had come back inside. Or she would have if not for Nadin banging into her as he rushed out, knocking loose her grasp on her invisibility.

"What are you *doing*?" she seethed, turning herself invisible as soon as she got her breath back.

"It was the fairy—"

"Got it!" cried Loram from inside the cell. She held a... hand? A fake hand, from the looks of it as she carried it out, and a disturbingly realistic one at that.

"Do I want to know?" Adren asked.

Loram grinned. "Mayhap not."

Fairies.

"So..." said Nadin. "How are we getting out?"

Adren pointed with her thumb and Loram set an illusion to keep them all unseen. With a sigh of relief, Adren let go of her invisibility.

"You have no idea how much I wish you were around in the last town," she told Loram.

They left the prison with far more ease than anyone who wasn't supposed to be in a prison in the first place should ever leave it. They passed by the guards and, for a laugh, Loram made it so Adren couldn't see the illusion they faced and the two of them chuckled as the guards fought nothing.

Nadin didn't share their delight. He kept sneaking glances at Loram, fidgeting every time he did.

Adren wanted to tell him to calm down. Loram wasn't a human, after all. That, and paranoia didn't suit him.

FIVE

Nadin may have stared at Loram on the way to the fairy mound, but he soon directed his attention at the tunnels. The illusion protecting the path to them—ghostly trees that feigned to block the way of travellers—as well as the wall of mist that guarded the entrance had made him quiet, shy almost. But it was the tunnels that made him silent, made his eyes go round.

To the eyes of one who could see through illusion, the walls were stone, carved all over with intricate artwork and writing unlike anything humans had ever made. It curled around the shapes of animals, people, fairies. It wove in and around scenes with beings both familiar and strange. Whether it told history or myth or both could not be ascertained without knowing how to read the script itself, but it clearly told something. Something important enough to be hidden.

The other fairies that passed them by in the tunnels also gave him pause. They also slowed at the sight of him, gave him a real look, unlike the disinterested kind from strangers who pass each other in the street. He saw them and they saw him and it obviously unsettled many of the fairies, what they saw.

Inside the throne room, the illusions gave way to reality. The thrones were indeed formed from the roots of trees, the walls covered with more of these, but in between, in an almost playful dance with these roots, the carvings and writings continued their story. Or stories?

The creatures depicted in these were stranger still. Some were dark and terrible, with eyes like stars. Others were bright and beautiful, winged and like fire. Werewolves and other partly human forms stood among them and away from them, their actions often hidden by the roots that had reached down through the room and into deeper earth. It wasn't clear what they did to or with the humans and magical beings that stood, numerous beyond measure, among them.

And then the fairy monarchs spoke.

Adren wanted to drag Nadin along through the tunnels when they'd entered into the fairy mound. He kept stopping at the oddest moments, captivated by nothing on the walls, by the fairies around them. If he wasn't human—which became less likely with each passing moment— didn't he know what fairy mounds were like? Had he never seen a fairy before? It would explain why he knew so little of magic and how it worked. If he had fairy blood, it must have come from his grandparents—great-grandparents at most, or else she doubted he'd have the abilities he did. The more human added to the mix, the weaker the magic became. Unless another magical creature decided to tamper.

Still, she found his wonder embarrassing. Did he really have to stare so much? Even in the throne room, where she might understand his reaction, his attention went to all the least impressive parts of the room.

Of course, he might be seeing more than she could. But why? They had roots coming down from the ceiling, in the saints' names! Fairies liked to make reality more glamorous, not the other way around.

As they entered the throne room, Loram was allowed to go with them before the dais. The fairies in the room watched every step of their approach. Even Loram became subject to unreadable expressions that made Adren want to shiver.

On the thrones sat the king and queen, accompanied again by Iraem.

"We see your attempt has been successful," said the queen to Adren. And then, to Loram: "What of yours?"

Loram held up the fake hand. Now it was Adren's turn to stare.

"Well done. And we thank you, Adren, for your most excellent gift." The queen appraised Nadin. He sputtered something vaguely questionlike towards Adren, but the queen ignored this. "As for our end of the bargain..."

Utter silence fell around Adren. Utter silence and utter blackness, as though walls had risen from the floor around her. Before her stood Iraem, still and silent as the middle of winter.

From the floor beneath Adren's feet, magic snaked its way up and around her ankles. It laid itself along her legs, growing like a vine. She tried to move out from its power, but it had bound her feet and she couldn't lift them.

No matter. She had magic, too.

As the fairy spell continued to work its slow way up her body, Adren let the fire within her leak through her skin. She wasn't sure exactly how to let it combat the spell, so she brought it in contact with the fairy magic and hoped it would do something on its own. Considering how it had saved her from the potion maker's spell in Watorej, she had no doubt it would be able to protect her again without much direction.

Her magic and the fairy magic met like wood sparking into flames. Adren's magic ate away at the subtle spell around her, forming an ever-widening circle where she was free from its influence. She gave Iraem a fierce grin. Iraem lifted her head a fraction, the barest hint of a sly smile touching the edges of her lips.

Adren's grin dropped.

Until that moment, Adren had thought it a game and nothing more. But what she saw in Iraem's eyes gave her a different testimony. Iraem didn't see her as an equal. Didn't see her as an ally. Iraem was the hunter who had eased her prey into her trap and now had only to stop it from struggling. To her, it was a game. And not the kind Adren would ever want to lose.

The moment the illusion fell around Adren, several fairies attacked Nadin. Fairies have slight frames, slighter enough than humans that they could never defeat one in a purely physical struggle, and they knew it. While Nadin may have been able to fight off one or two of them, five were too many. He tried to fight them, but their collective strength held him down. Even his magic only caught them by surprise. The others around them suppressed his attacks before he had done more than bruise his attackers.

"I like this one," the king said to the queen. "He could be of use."

"Not too much use, I hope," remarked the queen.

"Why are you doing this?" asked Nadin. "What did I do to you?"

The monarchs exchanged glances.

"Must thou have done something?" asked the queen. "But, to answer thy question: we merely act in accord with our arrangement. Adren wanted a cure, we wanted thee. Now we have what we desire."

Nadin narrowed his eyes. A moment later, they went wide and it was as if the strength left his body. "She... she couldn't have..."

"I assure thee, she did."

"So why put an illusion around her?" Nadin asked, straightening.

"We prefer efficiency," said the king in a languid tone. "We deal with thee, while our daughter completes the rest of our arrangement in private." Then, to the fairies holding Nadin: "He bores us now. Remove him to his place."

As the fairies dragged Nadin away, he screamed to Adren to help him as if hoping he could break through the illusion. Even as the doors to the throne room closed, he screamed. But it was clear she could not answer him.

Though the magic that held Adren burned away at the touch of her own, Iraem raised her hands, palms up, and stone ties appeared. They wrapped themselves around Adren's body and legs, pinning her arms to her sides.

Except Adren knew an illusion when she saw one— no fairy could make something out of nothing—and she pressed her arms through and through and through and through…

These ties were thick, it seemed. She couldn't get her arms out of them. Why couldn't she get her arms out of them? The logical thing would have been to look down, but Adren knew that she wouldn't see the truth, no matter how clear it was.

And neither would she feel the truth. She may even be free already and only the fairies would know it until she could get away from their power. Iraem must have seen Adren realize this and her smiled deepened.

"So, you can use your illusions on me. Amazing." Adren put as much sarcasm as she could muster into that one word. Which was quite a bit, despite the circumstances. "Now that we're done with the small talk, what do you want? Is this some sort of test before you give me the cure?"

"I used to want a plaything, but Loram has been generous with me today. Now I want for nothing."

"So now you have Nadin. What does that have to do with me?"

"Oh, Nadin is my parents' plaything, not mine."

Adren swallowed. "I'm not human."

"And neither will you let me call you thee. So here we are."

Adren didn't know how to respond. Her truth sense had remained silent all through her first meeting with the monarchs, but that couldn't have meant anything. Fairies were magical beings, and magical beings didn't deal with others in such an underhanded way. They just didn't.

"What about the cure?"

"I believe you were the only one to say anything of it."

That couldn't be true. Every detail of Adren's first meeting with the monarchs raced through her mind. Every word spoken. She had asked for the cure and they had agreed, hadn't they? Perhaps not explicitly, but it was understood.

"I notice you have left behind our dialect entirely with me," Iraem said. "Am I meant to take that as an insult? Surely one who grew up with fairies, as you claim, would hold tighter to it in times of duress. Or did you lie to me about that? I shall not hold it against you. It shall be our secret, my dear plaything."

Perhaps Adren had missed a detail. Something that, once remembered, would make everything make sense again. Iraem's spell now gone, Adren stopped her magic's flow and did her best to ignore the weight of the stone ties as she turned and walked away.

The walls around her vanished, revealing that, of the

three who had stood before the dais, only Adren remained. She turned to face the monarchs, but they had also gone. All that were left were Iraem and a large number of other fairies.

"Where is Loram?" Adren demanded of Iraem.

Iraem only shrugged.

The fairies around them came at Adren, both with magic and physical force. She fought them off as best she could, and slowed their attack. Stopping it, on the other hand...

They grabbed her and gagged her with magic that held firm with a collective force her own couldn't break. One of them hit her and everything went dark.

Nadin swore at the fairies as they pulled him through the tunnels, using a wide variety of words which were all the more shocking coming from him. Several he'd learned from Adren. Most had not passed his lips before this day.

The fairies hauled him into a dank, dark part of the mound, threw him into a room little larger than a hole, and laughed as they closed the door. He slumped in the corner.

"Great. Now I'm in prison again."

Around him, fairy illusions and magic shimmered, both inside his new cell and outside it. And along the door. Nadin perked up and went over to it.

"Hmmm..." With a frown, he tried the door. Said door refused to cooperate. Nadin's frown deepened as his gaze ran up and down the lines of magic that flowed within the wood.

When Adren woke, she found herself in a room so small she couldn't stand or lie down with her legs straight. The damp walls smelled of dirt and rotten wood. The door, which she rushed to the moment she saw it, was locked and only let in light through what few chinks there were in the wood. She couldn't see anything more.

Saints and all the gods besides.

In the name of all the saints and the mothers who bore them.

Gods in hell, with their stinking breath, may they eat the bowels of the fairies responsible for this and spit the masticated remains back into their faces so they can die by choking on their own fetid leavings. May the gods' curses reach their firstborn and cast them down into the pit of hell to entertain the divine who are never satisfied. May the fairies watch this as they choke, may they know with more horror than they have ever experienced in a lifetime that they signed their sentence the moment they decided to do this... this...

Adren buried her head in her hands.

This couldn't be real.

They had lied to her. Fairies—magical beings—had lied to her. They'd lied to her, attacked her, and imprisoned her. And for what? So Iraem could have a plaything.

What if Iraem hadn't met Adren, hadn't decided she wanted to keep Adren for her toy? Loram hadn't gone into the prison for Nadin. She'd used Adren to get in so she could retrieve the wooden hand, probably to get back into the good graces of the monarchs. No wonder the prison had a fairy-proof barrier. Adren had thought it just a precaution against their mischief, but now she could see it had been to keep the fairies from getting back that hand. The obvious question of why anyone would want it aside, Adren had been used. Kidnapped. Lied to.

No, no, no, no! This couldn't be real! She pounded on the door until she almost bled. She wanted to let her magic loose, gods eat the consequences.

She wished she'd never let Nadin go into town in the first place.

Saints, it was all her fault.

With that thought, she curled up in that wet hole and rocked as she did all she could to keep the pinpricks of tears from escaping her eyes. The river of her emotions poured through to the unicorn, alarmed it. It wanted to come, to comfort and, for one insane moment, Adren wanted it, too. Until she remembered exactly how many fairies there were in this mound. The unicorn would never be able to stand against them.

Would it need to? Iraem had implied that she justified her actions by Adren not counting herself a magical creature. Terrible as the fairies had been to Adren, they couldn't possibly be so evil that they would harm the unicorn.

No! They couldn't be evil. Going back on a promise— that was something humans would do. Not fairies. There had to be something else, something Adren couldn't see yet. So she let the unicorn come, praying that its presence would be what the fairies needed to show her what their true purpose was.

Time in the hole passed in a jolting, sideways fashion. Adren would fill with a desire to give in to all that boiled within her, a desire so strong she almost couldn't control it. Somewhere outside of that was the rest of the world. Somewhere outside of that was the grime of dirt against her fingers and that damp, earthy smell. And then her body would relax, turn to normal again as she reminded herself that the unicorn was coming, that the fairies would recognize it for what it was, and that she would be released. Except, as she thought of the fairies and what they'd done to her, it would start all over again. That sick feeling in her stomach would return and it would be all she could do again to keep from losing herself to it and all it implied. Time slowed, stretched out thin and hot, and the next bout of relaxation was always too short to compensate.

But the unicorn was coming, so she held on. She held on as it approached through the forest, as it came so close she almost thought she could hear it in the tunnels, as it...

As it blazed through with pain and fear that sent claws through the connection. Saints and all the gods besides, that *hurt*. Adren's forehead tingled with it. The unicorn drew back from whatever the source was, confused.

"Come on, come one," Adren said. A minor setback, only. Something humans had left. It had to be that.

The unicorn plunged to her again, only for the pain to connect, worse this time. It tangled through the connection in vinelike tendrils. Terror rose, an ocean to flood all else, and the unicorn ran.

Away.

SIX

"There has to be something I'm not seeing," Nadin said. "It can't be that simple. They do know I can see magic, right?" He squinted. "Sometimes."

He sent out some exploratory tendrils of his own magic. They wiggled in and around the door, poked at the enchantments in it. He scratched his head. Tapped his chin.

"Huh. But there's no use trying to escape while everyone's awake." With a nod, he settled himself on the floor and took a nap.

Sometime later, Nadin yawned, stretched, opened his eyes. He then sat in place for several moments before blinking and shaking his head.

"You know, I would have liked for this to be a dream. Just this once."

Stretching again, he stood and peered at the door to his cell. Before his nap, while the tunnels outside had been dark compared with the rest of the mound, they'd still had enough light for someone to walk along them without tripping themselves. Now, even that light had dimmed and all that remained visible were the curtains of illusion and the occasional thread of an enchantment.

Nadin hummed to himself as his magic reached out to meet the enchantment on the door. The magic fiddled with the threads for a moment before they unravelled. With a smile, Nadin tried the door. It opened. He laughed, but cut himself short by clamping a hand over his mouth. Only after he poked his head out and checked the tunnels did he relax again and chuckle instead.

Under his breath, he said, "I cast more complex ones on Lord Watorej's motorized carts. For safety, but still." He paused. "Adren—" His jaw clenched. "This is probably a trap. Which means I really should stop talking to myself." Taking a deep breath, he nodded. Opened his mouth. Evidently thought better of the idea, closed it, and headed out.

The tunnels of a fairy mound are not designed with the casual visitor in mind. They are created as if grown, and so the only logic they have in their design is a haphazard one at best, although some are better marked than others. Growing up in a mound, one would learn its layout through experience. A new visitor to the mound, on the other hand, would need either a guide or a stupendous amount of luck to get to their intended destination on the first try.

As a result, even with his ability to see the magic of both the tunnel he walked and those beyond, Nadin spent a great deal of time getting nowhere. He stopped, turned around and around all while counting under his breath. With a frustrated groan, he said, "There are too many of them!" Pause. "Oh, but what if…"

In some places, the illusions were thicker than in others. In some places, the enchantments covered a much larger area. One place in the mound had both. Nadin headed off towards it.

The enchantment, as it turned out, coated the entire surface of a door, and the room on the other side held layer upon layer of illusion. It also held the source of muffled weeping.

He paused mid step. The weeping died down, gave way to shuddery breaths. Sometimes, it would stop completely, creating a deafening silence until a gasp started the whole stumbling cycle all over again.

Nadin took a hesitant step towards the door. Whoever was behind it continued as if they hadn't heard him. He took another step. And another. When he was close enough to reach out and touch the enchantment, the person inside stopped weeping, instead doing what sounded like scrabbling away from the door. Nadin winced, then sighed.

"Are you all right in there?"

"Nadin?" It was Adren's voice.

Getting burned wouldn't have made him draw back as fast as he did. Arms shaking, he balled his hands into fists, but he didn't speak.

"If you're an illusion, then you're an illusion. But if you aren't, please. I need to get out of here."

Nadin took a deep, careful breath before answering. "Why would I help you, when you gave me to the fairies?

Like a thing! As part of an agreement." His voice was hushed, intense and quivering with raw emotion.

"Gods," Adren said in a small, small voice.

"Didn't think I'd find out, did you?"

"It's not that, it's... this is all my fault."

Nadin snorted. "Yes. That's exactly how it is." He turned to go.

"No! Wait! Don't leave me here!"

"Why not? You *gave me* to the fairies. After I helped you in Watorej, after I stayed with you while you had those attacks, you decided to trade me away. And for what? Did you even think of anyone but yourself in all—" He clapped his hands over his mouth.

"I did it for the unicorn," Adren whispered. "They promised me a cure. Then they did this." When Nadin didn't respond, she continued. "I thought that, if you were part fairy, they wouldn't treat you badly."

"And if I was human?"

"You know what I think about humans."

Nadin threw his hands down and paced in front of the door. "What if I am human?"

Silence.

He chewed his lip. "I hate you for doing this, you know that?"

"I understand."

"So why would I help you?"

"Because it's the right thing to do."

The tunnels were so quiet it was as if the roots listened to them. Nadin sighed.

"Fairies are selfish, you should know that. They don't give unless they know they're going to get something better."

"*Humans* are selfish, id—" She bit back the word. "And don't go telling me what fairies are like. I grew up with them. I know what they're like, and they're not like that."

"Well, maybe not your fairies," muttered Nadin. "But other fairies are. A lot of them, in fact. I thought you'd know better."

"Nadin," Adren's voice shook. "I don't care. I just want to get out of here. You got out. Please, help me."

"Fine." He scrubbed at his forehead. "Fine. I'll get you out."

In a few moments, he'd unravelled the enchantment and opened the door. Inside illusion lay thick around Adren, one that made the room seem like a cramped hole in the dirt. In truth, she stood, hunched to fit the space she thought she had, in a fine, spacious room.

"What is *wrong* with these fairies?" Nadin said under his breath, shaking his head.

When Nadin opened the door, Adren was relieved to find the tunnel dark enough to hide her face. He had most certainly heard her crying, but if he could see her face, then he would be able to see the tear stains on her cheeks. He'd be able to see her eyes. If she had to meet his eyes right now, the veneer of composure she'd cultivated inside her would break and everything underneath would come free. She couldn't pretend he hadn't heard her. She couldn't pretend he hadn't seen her.

Because it was so dark and because Adren couldn't see the illusions, she kept a hand on Nadin's shoulder as she followed him. Touching him while she was still so fragile caused every muscle in her body to tense, so much that she had to consciously relax in order to walk without discomfort.

Their footsteps echoed strangely in those tunnels. Or did they? Did Nadin hear it differently? Adren hoped he didn't. She wanted something real after all these illusions. At least none of the fairies would try to stop them. Fairies and their sleep—still, Adren kept expecting something, anything to happen. After all, *something* had hurt the unicorn. As they worked their way through the tunnels, Adren tried to keep track of where the unicorn had met... whatever had hurt it. She couldn't remember the exact position, but she had a rough idea based on where the unicorn now waited.

By the time they found their way out of the mound, the position of what stars were visible between the jagged teeth of tree silhouettes indicated almost half the night had passed. The moon, a thin slice at this time of month, had already set. Adren took her hand from Nadin's shoulder and shivered. They had entered the area she thought was where the unicorn had been attacked. Part of her thought telling Nadin about it would help them avoid whatever was out there. Another part hoped against all hope that the unicorn had come up against something momentary, some sort of random happenstance that she couldn't possibly connect to the fairies.

The path to town opened up before Nadin a few steps at a time. Adren hurried to walk next to him and all the hair on her body rose before she could stop herself from setting foot on the path. Magic shot through her the moment her shoe connected with the bare dirt. It was like walking into a wall, except the wall was lined with prehensile vines that sought out her skin and burrowed under it to snake through her veins.

Her magic rose to protect her, white-hot and wild, but the veins had endless power behind them. She could tell, even if they hadn't called on their full strength yet, that behind them lay a vast reservoir. The fury of her magic would last for only so long, while whatever that magic was would last and last. Growing bit by patient bit, it would subdue her magic as if it were a child having a tantrum and this spell were the parent come to discipline it. She had to get away, but something had gone wrong between her mind and body. It wouldn't do what she wanted.

Adren cried out.

Nadin turned. Before she could shape the words to tell him what was happening, he grabbed her by the hand and pulled. She stumbled after him. The magic bristled and sped up to touch her mind. There, it seemed to have found what it wanted. Ignoring the dark place and Adren's connection to the unicorn, it shuffled through everything else as her magic fought it with helpless rage. Still, the distance between the invading magic and the source of its power kept growing. As it did, the magic's patient purpose began to warp under the pressure of her inborn defense. Not break. Alter. Unclear as its original intent was, Adren wasn't sure this was better.

Her legs fell out from under her. They simply stopped

responding. Nadin almost fell, too, but he steadied himself in time.

"Adren! Adren, hold on, it's going to be fine."

Adren.

Hold on, Adren.

Hold on.

The twisted magic found its hold and dug right into the tissue of it. Pain ran through Adren's bones, deep in the marrow.

There was a little girl dancing.

There was a fire.

There was a sword.

As Adren collapsed, Nadin rushed to her.

"Adren! Adren!"

She didn't respond. Nadin grabbed his hair and groaned. They still hadn't gotten to the end of the path and, thin as it was, the thread that connected the spell in Adren back to its source at the start of the path hadn't broken yet. The spell itself ran all through her, a beacon to all who had eyes to see and who cared to look in that direction. Nadin picked her up. She muttered something, but so quiet that the words were incomprehensible.

"Not again." As he rushed on, something darted through the trees. He flinched, but kept going. The something might have been a deer, from its size, except its coat was too pale.

The unicorn stepped out in front of Nadin, horn lowered. He stopped.

"I'm not hurting her," he said in a gentle, if strained, voice. The unicorn snorted and stamped the ground. "Please, I promise I'm not. I'm trying to help her." He circled the unicorn, step by careful step, towards its flank. The horn followed.

As soon as he'd gotten far enough that the unicorn couldn't just turn its head, it danced away from him and angled its body in his direction more comfortably.

"No, don't do that," Nadin exhaled through his teeth. "I'm trying to put her on your back. Don't you see?" He illustrated as best he could while still holding Adren. "You can keep her safe that way, and we can walk faster."

Although the unicorn pawed the ground, it did so less fiercely. Again Nadin went around it.

"It's all right. You know me," he said in soothing tones. As he carried Adren to the unicorn's side, he kept reassuring it. So long as he remained slow enough, it let him come. The moment he moved too fast, it stomped its hind legs and danced away. Nadin took this in stride, pausing until the unicorn calmed and he could continue again.

Which would have made him seem the pinnacle of patience if not for how often he grimaced and glanced back at the mound whenever the unicorn became agitated. Still, it was to his credit he didn't try to pass by and disregard the unicorn entirely. He might not have survived that decision.

Getting Adren onto the unicorn's back proved awkward. She had enough awareness to grab onto its mane, but the strength of her grip wavered and her balance overall left much to be desired. In the end Nadin sort of draped her over the unicorn and walked alongside it, holding one of Adren's arms to keep her from sliding off.

As they went, the thread of magic that stretched along behind them became thinner and thinner until it finally broke. The moment it did, Nadin took a deep breath, his chest rising and falling in an even rhythm for the first time since Adren had cried out.

They followed the edge of town, far enough that the unicorn remained hidden in the trees, close enough that the occasional enchantment could be seen. Troublesome as fairies were, they did make things humans couldn't usually get. One house in particular had quite a number of enchantments in and around it, not all of them fairy-made, but all of them enough to drown out the sight of the spell in Adren. It lay near the edge of the town, on the side farthest from the fairy mound and, as Nadin approached it, its walled yard became visible.

"If only we could get in..." Nadin scratched his head. He led the unicorn around the wall until they came to a gate. "Uh." Watching Adren, he let go of her arm and paused, both hands at the ready. When she didn't fall, he went to the gate and tried to open it. This met resistance, but he peered over the top and reached down to undo the latch.

Gate now open, Nadin was about to turn back when a woman came out into the yard, lamp in hand. She was the one from the market who had argued with her brother over egg placement.

"You!" The woman stepped back, turned as if for flight.

"No, please! She needs help!"

At Nadin's cry, the woman paused. She watched as he led the unicorn into the open. It quivered, but turned until the woman could see Adren.

"Did you do this to her?" asked the woman, eyebrow raised despite being visibly unsettled.

Nadin shook his head. "The fairies did. Could you help her? And put the unicorn somewhere it won't be seen? I need to go back and get them to break the spell. Please."

The woman sighed. "I'll help. But don't go tonight. You can stay here, get some sleep. Don't go until you're rested."

"I'll help them get settled, but I need to go back before morning—"

"Nonsense. You may not feel it yet, but I can tell you're about to drop right where you stand, and you will if you're not careful." She beckoned to him.

"Were you the one who sent the soldiers after me?"

"Yes."

"Will you do it again?" His voice was soft, without accusation.

"Only if I need to." Nadin slumped. "But I don't need to tonight. I have other things to attend to. You, for instance. My name is Denyeh."

"Denyeh!"

"What? What's wrong with my name?"

"Nothing," said Nadin as he made a placating gesture. "The guards mentioned you. You're the one who made the barrier around the prison, right?"

"Yes." She narrowed her eyes.

"They're going to need another one. Adren took it down

to get me out of there." A sad smile touched the corners of his lips. "My name's Nadin. Thank you for helping us."

Denyeh paused but, with a sigh, beckoned again. Nadin followed her in, bringing the unicorn and Adren with him.

A jumble of sensations. A little girl laughing. Speaking. Somewhere there was a fire and a man... weeping? No, he wasn't weeping by the fire. That was somewhere else. Or maybe that was all together, all at once?

The new dress twirled beautifully as she danced and her fair hair spun with it, at times resting a moment to hide the whiteness of her face.

Magic. There was magic.

Oh, gods, there was that sword. The sword, held by a man whose face Adren could not make sense of. He swung the weapon down towards her until her forehead burned. She could hear little-girl screaming, but the man's voice cut through it, pleading even as it shook with anger. The words all mashed together, an incoherent stream of deformed sentences.

Run!

Running.

Running.

A misstep as the whole world shook, as if someone below the earth had gone into a rage and beaten its foundations. Everything shaped oddly after that. And more magic, still shaking the earth.

Hold on, Adren, hold on.

A panicked unicorn and a little girl ran, swallowed up in

the darkness of the trees.

At this point, it was as if Adren's head were shoved underwater, the whole event made to waver into nothing as she gasped for breath. Until, piece by piece, the whirling black revealed a kaleidoscope, a sword, flight. Plunge. Chaos. Pain. Fear.

Plunge.

Plunge.

Plunge.

Fragments of Nadin's and other voices worked their way through, pieces of glass that hung in the air at odd intervals. She tried to speak, to do what they asked. She didn't know how well it worked, or if it worked at all. The spell had taken hold of her senses, overlaid what it had gathered from her mind on them such that she couldn't tell what was real and what was memory.

She had no choice but to trust Nadin now.

SEVEN

Once he'd made sure the unicorn and Adren would be safe with Denyeh—and once Denyeh had made sure he'd at least eaten—Nadin went back to the forest. The morning air still held the night's lingering chill, a chill which Nadin hadn't reacted to while Adren was still in danger. He did now, though, rubbing his arms as he walked briskly. He winced when he rubbed the scratches Adren had made, back before either of them had entered the town.

The magic of fairies dotted the forest around the mound, and not just along the pathway. Nadin moved with caution through the trees, avoiding the path. It wasn't simply magic that hung in the air like will o' the wisps throughout the forests—the fairies themselves were out, too. Despite his care, one followed him from behind, swift when he was not, and taking a meandering path that could have been random as much as if it could have been purposeful.

Nadin followed his own twists and turns as he wove around trees to keep out of sight of fairies. Except for the few who followed their pathway, their locations had no order to them. Some clumped together, some were alone. Most made their way back to the mound.

Nadin had stopped behind a tree while a group of fairies walked past when his follower caught up with him.

The fairy sent a line of magic at him as he stared, eyebrows raised. He ducked the moment he collected himself, and the magic singed a few hairs as it whizzed past.

"Loram?"

She grimaced. "How did you get out?" A spell worked its way through the ground and up the tree behind Nadin before it lashed out at him. This one he didn't dodge in time, fascinated as he was the by glow of magic in Loram's satchel. The spell knocked him over and Loram rushed to grab him. They struggled, Loram sending spats of magic out even as she tried to immobilize his limbs. Nadin reached for the satchel as he defended himself.

As soon as he grabbed it, Loram pulled away and the struggle turned to one over whatever was inside. Both of them scrabbled at the satchel. Nadin, thanks to his human blood, managed to keep Loram at bay long enough for his hand to close on the object. He wrenched it from Loram and retreated a few paces.

The wooden hand lay in his grasp, full with a magic that flowed in strange configurations. Not a spell in wait, not an enchantment. Nothing like the magic another being might hold.

With a cry, Loram lashed out at him, both with magic and with her fists. Most of it landed. None of it left a mark.

She fell back.

"What kind of magic is this?" asked Nadin.

"I could ask you the same question, since you seem to be using it."

"Me?"

"How long have you known? Was it your fairy family who told you about it?"

Nadin blinked. "Told me about what? I have no idea what you're talking about."

Loram stared at him with an expression of bitter envy. "That I do not believe."

"I really don't," said Nadin with a shrug. He frowned, giving the fake hand a thoughtful look. As he did, Loram sent out magic through the ground, this time outwards, towards the other fairies. It went in streaks, like shooting stars below the earth, only there a moment before it vanished. Nadin raised his head when the last flew to their targets, one of them quite close. He met Loram's eyes, which had grown hard, and gulped.

And ran.

With a shout, Loram pursued him, as did the nearby fairy. As he ran, Nadin clutched the wooden hand to his chest as if it were the most valuable thing he had ever held. He stumbled and fell a few times in the undergrowth, but his grip never loosened. Loram never stumbled. Neither did the other fairy. Each time Nadin did, they gained on him, Loram especially.

Nadin gasped for breath as he skirted the edge of the town. His stumbles became more frequent. Soon, Loram had grown close enough that she only needed him to falter once more before she could reach out to grab him. The other fairy pursued him from not far behind her, but still far enough to be hidden by the trees.

Chickadees called out their name as the three neared their perches, only to fly off in an explosion of wingbeats. Nadin jumped at the sound, set his foot down wrong, and fell forwards into the underbrush. He struggled to rise, and Loram was reaching, reaching...

Behind her, the other fairy sent a blast of magic that knocked Loram over. The smell of smoke hung in the air where it hit her.

"Hinor!" she cried. "Not *me*." Crackles of the fairy's spell closed in around her, stinging her every time she got too near.

The other fairy, a boy, came into sight. While Loram tried to pick herself back up, he shooed Nadin away. Nadin hesitated, but that made the boy's motions only more agitated.

"Run," he mouthed.

As Nadin raced away, the boy cried apologies to Loram. He really hadn't been aiming for her. He promised he hadn't.

When Nadin arrived, flushed and out of breath, at Denyeh's house, he headed straight for Adren. Denyeh had put her in her own room. Holding out the fake hand, Nadin pointed its fingers towards Adren, who tossed on the bed.

Her muscles strained against nothing; she kept clenching and unclenching her fists. A sheen of sweat covered every bare part of her skin. As for her breathing, the motion of her chest was so erratic it wasn't clear how often she was able to fill her lungs, if at all. Denyeh, who had followed Nadin into the room, stared at the hand as he caught his breath.

"Is that real?"

"No." Nadin rapped his knuckle against it. "It's just wood. But it has magic in it of some kind, which might be able to help her."

"I swear I'll never understand fairies."

Nadin shrugged, returned his focus to the fake hand. His magic poked at it, nibbled along the edges of what it contained.

"I wonder if I..." The hand shuddered as his magic slammed into it. At which point the magic under the wood began to leak from the fingers. Leaking turned to flowing. Flowing turned to pouring. The hand was becoming empty at an alarming rate. "Hell."

"What?" Denyeh's eyes went round.

"I, uh, might have let loose all the magic in this thing. Hold on. I have to stop it before it goes crazy." Holding the wooden hand with both of his flesh-and-blood ones, Nadin strained as his magic tried to force itself through the flow of the strange magic that now poured over Adren.

"Can I do anything to help?"

"Maybe. Yes. Can you put a barrier around this hand? Uh. Quickly?"

Now completely covered in magic, Adren moaned and shifted on the bed. Her breathing had calmed, but she still tangled the blankets with her movement.

"I might be able to. Give me a moment." Denyeh hurried

from the room.

"Wait, what? Where are you going?" Nadin's eyes bulged as he stared back at the now Denyeh-less spot. "Denyeh!"

Frantic now, his magic threw itself against the outpouring from the wooden hand, widening to capture it, narrowing to pierce it, wedging itself into the flow. The hand's magic didn't appear to appreciate being forced and opted to shove Nadin's away each time. Finally, he covered the hand with his and sent his magic out from his skin to wrap around the object. The wooden hand shook and leapt as the magic tried to find a way out, but he held his grip steady and didn't let go. Before long, the shaking stopped and the hand settled back to the way it had been, albeit more empty than full. As Nadin let go of the hand, Denyeh returned.

"I thought I had something that might help, but it looks like it's nothing more than a saint's gauntlet." Her eyes went to the wooden hand, then to Nadin.

"Saint's gauntlet?" he asked.

"Oh, it's just a phrase. There's a story around here that one of the saints had gauntlets that he wore when they fought the gods and locked them into hell. As a result, the gauntlets supposedly gained the ability to make the wearer invulnerable, and could give them access to powerful magic. But the saint lost them on the way to heaven because he followed the advice of a demon and took them off when he stopped to drink. They fell, one into the water and the belly of the dragon that lived underneath, and the other to the earth. I just meant I lost the thing that would have helped stop this magic from getting everywhere."

"Do the gauntlets really exist?"

Denyeh shrugged. "You know how it is with the lives of the saints. Stories pop up here and there. Who can say how much of it is true? Anyways. You seem to have managed on your own." They turned to Adren. She had become still and as close to relaxed as she ever got, but nothing more had happened.

"I hope so... How long do you think it will take for us to find out how badly I did?"

"How badly?" Denyeh laughed. "You went to the fairy mound and came back with a fake hand full of magic. Yes, you spilled it all over her rather inelegantly, but that's minor. I know a thing or two about fairy spells and cleaning up after them. It comes with living in a town so near their mound."

"Oh, good," said Nadin as he breathed a sigh of relief. "I was trying so hard to fix this. I don't know what I would do if I'd hurt her just because I had no idea what I was doing."

From the bed there was a grunt as Adren shifted and opened her eyes. Both Denyeh and Nadin held their breaths.

"Nadin," said Adren with a frown. "Who in the names of all the saints is she?"

He grinned.

Before he gave her a proper answer, Nadin grabbed Adren up into an unnecessarily tight hug.

"I was so worried about you!"

Adren coughed. "My lungs would like to work right now. If you would let them."

"Oh, sorry." He let her go. "How do you feel?"

She took stock. Aside from a few lingering threads, the spell had dissipated. The memories had receded back into their appropriate places in her mind. Her body seemed to be responding properly. She tried wiggling her toes, which was successful except for a knee spasm towards the end that sent it shooting up and whacking Nadin's arm.

"Ow."

Good spasm.

"Everything's fine. Now. Who's she?" Adren jerked her thumb at the woman in question, and the reason why she wasn't going to say anything about what had happened inside the mound yet.

"I'm Denyeh," she said.

"She helped take care of you during the night and while I went back to the mound."

"You *what?*" The wooden hand resting on her stomach suddenly registered. "Oh, gods, Nadin, did you do what I think you did?"

"I didn't go inside the mound. Loram found me before I could and, well, I took the hand from her. Well. We fought and I grabbed at her satchel. She kept zapping me with magic, which hurt, but I was almost able to get my hand inside the satchel when she realized what I was doing, so then we fought over that for a while..."

Adren waved at him to shut up. "Fine. Fine. Why is it on me?"

"Oh. Sorry." He picked the hand up. "It had magic in it, which I used to help break the spell on you."

Gods in hell, Nadin.

"And you couldn't use your own magic because...?"

Nadin's mouth rounded. "I... I didn't think of that. I've never dealt with anything that powerful before."

Adren glared.

"Is there anything I can do right now?" asked Denyeh. "Food? Drink? Instantaneous transmission of information from one mind to another?" Funny.

"Don't make me like you," Adren said with a grimace. She wanted to leave it at that, but she hadn't eaten since yesterday afternoon, and her stomach had started to complain. "I could eat something."

Denyeh nodded and made a graceful exit.

"Nadin, about—"

"There's a really weird magic in this hand though," Nadin said, voice lowered. "I've never seen anything like it."

"So you used it on me?" Saints and all the gods besides, what had he been thinking? Didn't he *know* how unpredictable magic could be if you didn't have proper control over it? Maybe he did.

Still, it had worked, and that was something.

And he was right, it *had* been unusual. The man had swung his sword down yet again when it was as if a rush of water had flooded down on her. It hadn't been like what she felt forced under between each round of memory. Clean, clear water. Water with starlight in it. It came around her, almost as if it had known she was in pain, and buoyed her up through it. She had breathed it in, and it had filled her with warmth, but through into the depths of her being to give her strength.

It had reached to the dark place in her mind, too, but she'd balked at that, afraid of what it might release. And though this magic shouldn't have been affected by her, it pulled back from the dark place to focus on the spell instead. The spell had shaken in the face of it, but it fell upon the twisted vines like the slow roll of the ocean and they dissolved beneath it. Most of them, at least. The magic had swept through and had gone before it could finish its work, leaving Adren cold and shaking in its wake.

"...weird that it wasn't in the hand before," Nadin was saying. Adren brought her attention back to the situation at hand. Hand. She groaned.

"Did something happen?" asked Nadin, leaning forwards. He wasn't angry. Or, if he was, he hid it well. He should be angry about what happened in the mound.

"Just a bad pun." And a throbbing in her forehead. She rubbed it. That sword... She sat up. "The sword!"

Nadin started. "The what?"

"The sword. I remember the sword coming down at me. It didn't go away this time."

"You mean...?"

"Yes, the sword you said I'd mentioned during those fits. I remember it. I kept seeing it happen, over and over again, until the spell was gone. Everything was a mess at first, and then there was a man with the sword and he swung it down at me and my forehead would start hurting. And then I'd be running with the unicorn until I was shoved down into the mess and it started all over again." She paused. "My forehead still hurts, though."

"What do you think it means?"

"It's a memory. It doesn't mean anything. It just is." She bit her lip. She hadn't meant to imply...

"You must have been really young when it happened."

It was all he said.

It was all either of them could say. Someone banged on the door before Adren could put the pieces of her reply together. She got out of bed and they both listened as Denyeh answered the door.

"Oh, damn," said Nadin. "I recognize those voices. They're the soldiers that locked me up. She must have called them again."

Adren raised an eyebrow and refrained from commenting on the people he chose to help him when he was in trouble. Instead, she tapped him on the shoulder to get his attention and mouthed: "How do we get out?"

Without hesitation, he started off down the hallway. She grabbed his shirt and he stopped.

"What?" he whispered.

"Invisibility first."

"Oh."

Hand on his shoulder, like in the mound, Adren turned them both invisible and squeezed to let him know it was done. They made their way down the hallway like this, past Denyeh and the soldiers in the main room, and out a back door into a yard surrounded by a stone wall. The kind farmers might make from the rocks they found in their fields, only tall enough to reach above Nadin's head. In the yard, nudging the rough wooden gate, was the unicorn. At this sight, Nadin's shoulder got a lot more than a squeeze.

"Ow!" He wiggled out of her grasp and rubbed his shoulder.

"What is *wrong* with you?" Adren hissed. The unicorn trotted up to her and nibbled at her ear, which dampened the effect somewhat.

"I had to put you on its back," Nadin whispered. "I couldn't carry you all this way. And then Denyeh showed up and there wasn't time to keep it hidden."

"There are *soldiers* in the house right now, Nadin. With swords. I swear, if it was a good idea to punch you right now, I would."

"I'm sorry," he said, staring at his shoes. As if that would help. Gods, Adren hoped that only this Denyeh woman knew about the unicorn. If she'd told those soldiers…

"We'll talk about it later. Right now, we have to get away." The unicorn nickered and moved its nibbling to the top of her head. She gave it a gentle push back down, only for her arm to go rigid.

"Are you all right?" asked Nadin.

"I will be," Adren replied through gritted teeth. "Some bits of the spell are still hanging around." The only joint on her arm she could move was her shoulder, so she managed to get said arm back by her side, but it was awkward until her muscles loosened again. "So. Going now. Come on."

The three of them got to the gate and were about to unlatch it when an unearthly mist rolled through and over the wall. It filled the yard and became so thick that Adren could only see a few paces around her. Saints. The fairies must have been peeved that Nadin had stolen the fake hand from them.

"Fairy magic," Nadin whispered. "It's not real."

"Got that. Do you see any of them?"

"I don't think so..." His eyes narrowed. "Not close enough for me to tell, at any rate. The illusion makes it difficult."

"What do you mean?"

"Because of all the magic. Fog makes it hard to see physical things. This much illusion makes it hard to see magic things unless they're really obvious. Oh—" He stopped himself. But Adren already knew where his mind was going. Hers had already gotten there when he'd first mentioned the difficulty.

"The fake hand has obvious magic, doesn't it?"

Nadin nodded.

"Give it to me."

Reluctantly, he obeyed. The wood was smooth, smooth enough that Adren almost couldn't tell it didn't have paint on it. But there, beneath her fingers, she felt the faint lines of the grain. It was an amazing piece of work, really, if in poor taste. The colouring must have been from stain, and whoever had done it had taken care to make the result as realistic as possible. If she weren't holding it at that moment, Adren would have sworn it was real. It also felt lighter than a piece of wood its size should be. Interesting. Perhaps it was hollow? She cuffed Nadin with it.

"What were you *thinking*?" The hand let off a spark when it connected with Nadin, but it didn't seem to do any physical harm. Adren offered it back to him.

"I couldn't just leave you like that, could I?" he yelled, taking the hand.

"I'm glad you didn't. And that you didn't leave me in the mound."

"I should have."

Adren drew back as if she'd been slapped. Nadin sighed.

"It wasn't about you. The only reason I helped you was because I thought of the unicorn having no one to take care of it. And because of those attacks you get. Because watching them—" He clenched his hands into fists and took a deep breath. "Because watching what happened with that spell was like watching my mother's illness all over again, except this time I could do something." And, for the first time since they'd arrived in this town, the honeysuckle taste of Adren's truth sense spread over her tongue and filled her whole mouth with its sweetness. "Yet another reason to hate humans, I guess."

She didn't know what to say. This whole time, she hadn't considered how everything had been affecting Nadin. Of course he'd been concerned about her, that much was clear, and he'd been upset about the fairies. But, even though she knew about his mother's illness, had seen it first hand, she hadn't thought he would be struggling with memories of his own.

This was the moment where she knew she should say something comforting. Something empathetic. She had no idea what that might be.

"A human wouldn't have done everything you did to

help me."

Nadin only stared at his feet and frowned.

The mist had thinned above shoulder level, not enough to see the forest, but nearly enough. And in that mist was movement.

"Nadin, get down!" Adren pulled him behind the wall and down until his head was well below the thicker portion of the mist and pushed the unicorn out of sight. As for herself, she peeked over the top of the dense part, like a selkie watching above the waves, waiting for an interloper to pass.

For interlopers *had* come.

Fairies, but not like Adren had seen them in the mound. Out here in the mist, they had taken on the appearance of fairies from human legend: tall, unearthly, and beautiful. They stirred up the mist around them as they surveyed the town with cold, indifferent eyes.

Adren had never seen fairies look like this before, with jewel-toned eyes and shining black hair, so tall that they were visible from the waist up, wearing robes of rich silk dyed in vivid colour and decorated in the intricate detail Adren remembered from the walls of the fairy mound she'd lived in. They looked like the saints come to walk the earth, only wild and fey. And not kind. With the curls of mist all around them and the way they seemed to glide through it rather than walk, it was as if time had stopped.

She shivered, expecting them to see the wooden hand's magic at any moment and converge on it in their uncanny silence.

They didn't. They walked by without even the smallest hesitation.

She ducked under the mist.

"Nadin. Why aren't they coming here?"

"Because we emptied the magic out of the hand. They can't see it."

"We?"

He shrugged. "I'd almost emptied it helping you, and the last bit got out when you hit me with it. Did you see the spark?"

"What kind of thing holds magic in it and then gets emptied like that?"

"Is that unusual?"

"Very."

And very impossible for the magic Adren knew about. Spells and enchantments involved finite amounts of magic that worked only according to the purpose for which they were set. Once that purpose ended or was made to end, the magic dissipated. Objects that could be used to allow humans to use magic usually housed spells or enchantments or both. The rarer of these objects allowed the user to channel magic the way a magical creature would.

The shorthand was that Adren *had* magic, or fairies *had* magic, but the truth was magic was everywhere; they only had greater or lesser ability to use it. When Adren's magic had surged from the dark place in her mind and filled her body, it wasn't that it had been hiding there and finally came out. Rather, her capacity to hold and direct magic, which had been blocked behind the dark place, had cleared out and the magic had rushed through, ready to use. The idea of an object that held a finite amount of magic with no specific purpose... it made no sense.

"Are you sure it wasn't a spell or enchantment and you broke it?" she asked.

"It definitely wasn't. I *told* you the magic was weird." He paused. "Um. Adren? We have a problem."

Adren raised her eyebrows and looked where Nadin was pointing.

The soldiers had entered the yard.

EIGHT

Nadin gaped.

"Get down!" Adren whispered. He obeyed, but the unicorn remained as it was. The soldiers drew their swords when they saw it, only the tips of the blades visible above the thick mist.

One of them opened his mouth to speak, but the unicorn screamed and they all went pale. Before Nadin could stand, Adren unlatched the gate and grabbed him, dragging him out of the yard. Through the mist they ran, the unicorn following, away from the town. As they did, Nadin answered Adren's questions about the soldiers, telling her about his whole experience from being accused as a spy to what the guards had said about the Saint's Gauntlet. At which point Adren demanded he explain and he told her what Denyeh had said about the saint who'd lost his gauntlets on the way to heaven.

It took some time for him to say all this. Running and talking at the same time is hard work and he'd also had little rest since escaping with the hand. They had to go for long periods of silence while he gathered himself to be able to speak, and these periods became longer and more frequent the longer they ran. But it was quite a ways from Denyeh's house to their destination, so he managed to get the whole story out before they reached it.

And reach it they did, Nadin gasping and holding onto a tree for support, Adren merely breathing hard. Somewhere along the way, the unicorn had parted ways with them and headed off deeper into the forest.

"I don't... understand... how you do it," he said. "Your legs are so... short."

"It comes from running from the law so often." She grinned. It was sudden, her smile. Brief, but bright as the sun peeking through the clouds on a dark day. Her smiles always hinted at a deep reservoir of happiness that she only seemed to tap into in the moments she was pleased with herself. This one was no exception.

When he'd recovered enough to stand upright by himself again, Nadin looked up. The beginning of a dirt pathway stood before him, with real trees on either side and illusory ones forming a dead end. "Wait. Why did we come here? Aren't the fairies going to be coming back when they realize the hand isn't in the town? Or am I missing something?"

"You're not missing anything." She paused. "Well. You haven't missed that. What do you know about fairies and pride?"

"Um. Nothing, I guess."

"How much *do* you know about fairies? And don't try

dancing around your ancestry, either. It's obvious by now that you're part fairy."

"No, I'm not!" His voice shook and the tips of his ears turned red. Adren raised an eyebrow.

"Then tell me where your magic comes from."

"You want to do this now? What about the fairies?"

"If this hand is important enough to them to search the town the way they're doing, they won't be back for a while yet. Why does it matter if I know?"

"Because if you know whether I'm human or not, you'll have already decided what you think of me. I'll have had no chance to... to earn my standing with you."

Adren's eyes widened.

"Say something!" said Nadin.

"I didn't think that mattered to you."

"Well, it does." He crossed his arms. "Can we... could we get back to talking about fairies?"

"All right," Adren said gently. "They care about their status with other fairies in the mound. And humans, too, but they don't talk about it like that. They can't bear to lose face, especially with fairies that have higher status than they do. And I bet that someone lost a lot of face when you stole the hand."

All through this, Nadin regarded her through narrowed eyes. "Why are you telling me this? You don't tell me things. We just do things."

"Because I need you to find Loram for me and negotiate a deal for her to save face." As he opened his mouth, she wagged a finger at him. "Don't tell me all the reasons why you can't. You have face with them, I don't. I was duped, but you got us out and then took from them the thing that caused this whole mess to begin with. More than that, if you're part fairy, you're a relative in their minds, however distant. Do you see?"

With a grimace, Nadin nodded.

"So..." Adren gestured towards the mound.

"Wait, what—? There? Why would she be in there?"

"I just told you why."

Outside the town, the mist had dwindled, though it still curled through the air. The forest was ghostly with it, and it seemed to move in the trees like a living thing. Illusion though it may have been, even the magic behind it hazed the air with twining threads that clawed their way along only to melt the moment they touched anything solid. Nadin bit his lip as he stared at it.

"What do I negotiate for?"

"Everything you can get." Adren's voice was hard, bladelike. "At the very least, I need the rest of this spell out of me, but try your hardest for the unicorn's cure, too."

"What if I can't find her?"

"Then, saints help us, we'll talk to the monarchs themselves."

At this, Nadin gave Adren a sidelong glance. Her jaw was set, her eyes narrowed. The happiness of her smile had vanished, leaving behind a coldness as terrible as the illusions the fairies had wrapped themselves in as they walked through the mist.

"I hope it doesn't come to that," he said quietly.

Adren couldn't risk getting caught in the spell again, and so stayed behind to deal with the soldiers, should they have followed. At least, that's what she told Nadin. The likelihood of the soldiers having followed this far without either her or Nadin noticing—or having followed at all after the unicorn's scream—was too low to be more than chance. Yes, she had to stay outside of the mound for her own safety. No, she wasn't going to stand around waiting for Nadin. An undercurrent of rage over what the fairies had done had been building as they escaped Denyeh's house. That they would abuse her trust so easily, that they would harm both her and the unicorn with magic—such things were unconscionable. They had chosen their actions, and now they would face the consequences.

Her anger drew the unicorn to her again. It nickered, butted its nose against her, but it couldn't calm her. Let the two of them stand against the multitude, should it come down to that. Adren did not intend to lose.

Besides, it wasn't Loram she hated most. It was Iraem. With all that had happened, Adren now understood how Iraem had convinced the monarchs to hear Adren's case. Loram had gone to them, offering to earn back her position by getting them the wooden hand, and asking for help and the cure Adren wanted so the mission would succeed. The monarchs refused, their reason either or both of how bad the deal was or Loram's low status. After this, Iraem told them they didn't have to do anything about the cure if they'd let her take Adren instead. Adren couldn't decide whose idea it was for the monarchs to have Nadin but, in the end, the monarchs stood to gain both the wooden hand and Nadin, Iraem got Adren, and Loram gained her position back. As she made her case and they worked out the details, Iraem would have been stupid not to point out the greatest benefit of all: if this worked, the mound and the mound alone gained all.

If she hadn't done this, Loram and Adren would have rescued Nadin, Loram would have had her fake hand to bring back to the monarchs, and they all would have gone on their way. Adren could have gotten the unicorn's cure at another mound, now that she knew it was possible. Nothing else had to happen.

"Come on," Adren said to the unicorn when Nadin was out of sight. "Let's find that saintsall fairy that thought she could make me a toy."

Nadin didn't need to count his steps as he entered the mound. He didn't need to keep careful track of which turns he'd taken through a complicated system that involved crooking his fingers oddly. He could have saved himself the exertion. Towards the centre of the mound a number of fairies clustered together, too close for anyone to give an easy count based on their magic of anything other than "many." As Nadin made his way through the mound, one of these fairies broke off from the group and made its way towards him. Before long, Loram rounded the corner.

"You!" Magic leaked from her fingers.

"Wait, don't!" Nadin lifted his hands, palms to her. "I

want to make a deal with you."

The leaking stopped. "What kind of deal?"

"You want that hand back, right? I want that spell off of Adren, and the cure you promised her."

"I didn't promise her anything."

"I meant you as in *you*." He gave a vague hand wave. "All the fairies here. Don't the monarchs speak for them?"

"Sometimes." Loram crossed her arms. "So, you have the hand. You could get something for yourself, you know. I don't think I'd help someone who'd used me in a trade."

"I'm doing this for the—" Nadin clamped his mouth shut. "You know who she is, right?"

The only response Nadin gave was to narrow his eyes.

"The White Changeling?"

"Who?"

"She's a criminal. A thief, liar, double-crosser. She's hurt a lot of people, all of them human. I bet she thinks you're human, doesn't she? How long until she hurts you? How long until she hurts your family? Even if she learns what you are, that won't protect them from her."

"I know all that," Nadin said. "Well, not the White Changeling part. But the rest. And Adren's met the only family I really care for. She could have done all kinds of things then, but she didn't. She tried to help." He squared his shoulders. "Just like I try to help her."

"It won't end well for you."

"I don't see you doing anything." Strong as his words were, Nadin's hands trembled.

The fairy sighed. "That's not the—"

"Loram?"

A boy a year or so younger than Nadin ran around the corner. As soon as Hin and Nadin saw each other, they froze.

All the humans had left the streets of the town. Only fairies walked it. Fairies, Adren, and the unicorn. The lingering spell threads made this difficult, as they now clung to her legs and made them shake. Adren had a flash of doubt as to the wisdom of her plan but, seeing the fairies again as they strutted about in their pretentious illusions, she knew it was the right choice. To distract herself from the spell's effects and keep herself going, she imagined that all the fairies walked on rickety stilts that would fall over in a sudden breeze. She imagined herself as that breeze.

Of course, she wouldn't walk right up to a nearby fairy and attack them until she found Iraem. Despite how saintlike they appeared, Adren recognized several of the faces as those she'd seen inside the mound. So she kept her distance, searching for the one face she wanted most to find.

The part she found odd, though, was that none of the fairies came after her. If Iraem had wanted a toy so much, then wouldn't the search be for both Adren and the fake hand? And what about Nadin? And why didn't they seem to reach when she passed by? Perhaps the illusion magic masked her own, which would mean that her magic wasn't unusual enough to be clear in it. If that were the case, then she'd give a lot to know what kind of magic hers was in the first place. She'd come up with a lot of theories over the years. The most likely, up until now, had been that she'd been born human, but had been tampered with by some magical being or other. Except that would, by its nature, make her magic unusual. Now that she knew that wasn't the case, the only possibility she had left was that she was some sort of magical creature. But which? No humanlike magical creature she knew of could turn invisible.

There had been a human town near the fairy mound she'd grown up in, too, and she remembered going there when she was about eleven and playing with the children there.

"Who are you?" one girl with beautiful blue-black hair had asked her.

"Adren."

"Do you live with the fairies? My mom says you live with the fairies."

"Does that mean you're a fairy?" asked another girl.

"Ooo!" said a third. "Can you show us magic?"

The first girl gave an impatient flip of her hair. "You don't look like a fairy."

"I'm not a fairy, but I do live with them." At this point, Adren was reconsidering her decision to play with them. Until she had an idea. "But I can do this." She turned invisible.

Except for the one with the beautiful hair, the girls shrieked. Some of the boys came over to investigate. Adren became visible again and they cried out, telling her to do it again. So she did a few times, invisible and back.

"I bet you're great at hide and seek!" said one of the boys. Adren wasn't sure what that was, but she blushed anyway, and all the children made a commotion again, this time over how red she could turn.

When they had quieted down, the third girl blurted out, "But is your skin the same colour everywhere?"

"Isn't yours?" Adren crossed her arms.

"Well, yeah, but mine's normal."

Even now, years later, Adren winced. Skin too white, hair too light. Neither fairy nor human. And a new addition to the list: Loram telling her that her magic was broken somehow.

"So what are you?" the girl with the beautiful hair had asked.

"I bet she's a changeling!" said one of the boys.

"What?" Adren stepped back. She hadn't expected that.

"Yeah, you know," he said. "Kids the fairies swap out for their own."

"Fairies don't do that."

"I think we should call you the White Changeling," said the girl with the beautiful hair. She smirked. "Like a nickname."

"A nickname?"

"Yeah, people like nicknames."

Adren wasn't sure she liked this one. "I... I guess so."

"Great!" The girl tapped her on the shoulder. "You're it." The rest of the children had run away, squealing, and Adren had had no idea what was supposed to happen next.

NINE

"Why art thou here, Hin?" Loram put her hands on her hips. "I must needs finish this conversation. Return to the children."

Nadin opened his mouth and closed it again. Hin pinched the bridge of his nose. Sighed.

"Nay, I cannot. I lied when I told thee I sent my magic at thee in error—I did so purposely, for I believe him to be part of my family." His Breimic accent came through thick in his earnestness.

"Oh no," said Nadin, not quite inaudibly enough, and the fairies frowned at him.

"I would have proof of this," said Loram. She pressed her lips together.

"We only need a few words." He turned to Nadin. "What is thy name in full?"

"Nadin Frem."

"Nay, thine other name. Thy true one."

"Look, do we have to do this? Why is this important?"

Nadin's voice cracked.

"What are you hiding, Nadin?" Loram asked. Both she and Hin regarded him with a new air. He stepped back.

"How would you even know I was related to you out there in the forest?"

"Thou rememberest me not, but I was present when thy mother brought thee to see thy father's mother's family. My father was among those who spoke with thy mother that day."

"If that's the case, you can't have recognized me. That was ten years ago."

"Thy magic has not changed." The fairy boy's gaze was level, intense. He didn't blink, and his eyes didn't leave Nadin's face.

Nadin threw his hands into the air. "Fine! The name you're looking for is Neidim ib Frenzin. Happy?"

"See'st thou now?" Hin said to Loram. "He is of my family."

"I do."

"Aye, and we must needs tell them where he is."

"You don't need to do that just now," protested Nadin. "Please. I'll contact them when I'm ready."

Hin nodded. "Loram, I ask thee to help him."

"Knowest thou what sort of request thou makest of me? I have no lower to sink. The monarchs shall cast me out for acting against their will."

Even Nadin grew quiet at this. A fairy alone did not live long. After too much time away from other fairies, they would lose their strength. Their bodies would wither away, organs would fail. They wouldn't be able to use magic to help themselves—the nature of their magic was the reason this happened. Together, they were strong. Apart, they died. Those with enough human ancestry mixed in often didn't have this problem, or had it less fatally, but they were taught of it. Only after several generations without any more fairies involved and without any problems would a part-fairy child not know of the danger they might face.

"My family sent me here for more than a visit. They hear rumours of the misuse of the Demonic Vessel, and wish to know if they must needs find new keepers for it. Help and, even shouldst thou fail, they shall welcome thee among them with honour."

Loram snorted. "I *thought* thy visit suspicious. But no one listened when I said not to let thee here. Methinks it has turned to my benefit that they did so. I shall help."

"Is that all fairies care about?" cried Nadin. "Their benefit?"

No one spoke for a moment.

"Thou hast lived among humans too long," Hin observed.

Adren had just entered the market when three fairies, crowned with leaves and accompanied by four others carrying spears, passed her—the monarchs and Iraem. And though they seemed to take no notice of Adren, Iraem slowed and stopped. Adren, too, stopped, the unicorn beside her, her breath shallow. When the other fairies had left, a cruelly beautiful smile spread across Iraem's face.

"My little plaything has come to find me," she said.

"And has brought a friend." But as her gaze fell on the unicorn, her smile froze. "That isn't a unicorn. The magic is all wrong. How did you get it to look so much like one?"

A chill entered Adren. Even though the unicorn felt no alarm at the fairy's presence, she put a hand on its shoulder.

"It *is* a unicorn," said Adren.

"If so, it is a poor one. What did you think you would accomplish in bringing such a sad creature to me? Did you think I would fix it? Not I nor any of my kind holds such power."

Adren tightened her hand into a fist, but her voice did not betray what caused the unicorn to lower its horn at the fairy. "Loram and your parents seemed to disagree."

"Now, see, my dear toy, I tolerate some contradiction, but carry it out too long and you bore me. Which means I must teach you to be interesting."

Pale snakes arose from the mist around Adren. They encircled her, hissing. She laughed and took a step forwards to walk out of the illusion. That was a mistake. The snakes may have been illusion, but they housed a painful magic that bit deep enough into her skin that hers had to ward it off. In response, the unicorn's muscles bunched with fear—not enough that it would act yet, but enough that it set Adren's teeth on edge.

"That was a warning, plaything. Next time it will be worse. Next time, the marks will be visible."

The snakes separated Adren from the unicorn. When she'd tried to walk out of them, she'd taken her hand from the unicorn's shoulder, and now they rushed to fill that gap.

On the other side of that writhing wall, the unicorn rolled its eyes and stamped with its forelegs.

"You forget, Iraem. I am by no means helpless."

"No, I do not forget," said Iraem. "You are the one who has forgotten. You forget what I can see, what I know. To those who have not seen you, you hover on the edge of myth, and yet your deeds are known. Humans suffer at your hand, and yet humans only. Did you think that would escape notice? Did you think you would escape retribution?"

Adren's heart skipped a beat when Iraem mentioned what she could see. As for the rest of it, even though part of her said she should get the unicorn to attack, she couldn't stop from defending herself.

"Humans deserve all I have done to them; I have done nothing wrong."

Iraem laughed. "And who made you judge of them? Oh, how delightful you are, my pet. Of course you have done wrong."

"I have not!" But doubt slivered into her mind. Had she judged Iraem's actions wrongly? The monarchs had questioned Adren about her morals. Perhaps they had agreed to taking her not to own her, but to help her. They were magical beings after all. They knew the difference between right and wrong. And, much as Adren thought she knew the difference, she'd been mistaken before.

Would someone who wanted to train Adren to her benefit call her a plaything, a toy, a pet?

Iraem was a fairy.

Adren's forehead ached.

"You have worthy qualities, Adren. Allow me to teach you the use of them. What other purpose would I have with you? Why else would I have spoken on your behalf?"

All she and Nadin had planned to do in this town was sleep and eat. After Watorej, she had decided to go home and rest for a while. Three weeks of travel later, punctuated by attacks of that terrifying memory, and now knee-deep in a debacle with fairies to deal with, Adren almost welcomed the exhaustion that flooded her. It could be simple. She could stop fighting, get the unicorn to stop fighting. The unicorn! If she was exhausted, it must be, too. For the first time, she wondered if dragging the unicorn along with her had harmed it even more or, at the least, prevented it from any healing it might be undergoing, no matter how slow that may be. Gods, what had she been thinking, bringing the unicorn with her to face Iraem like this? It was only going to get hurt, and it was all her fault. They could wait a little longer to find its cure, if they needed. If it meant Adren would learn to treat it better.

"Don't—" Adren couldn't finish the sentence. She wanted to tell Iraem not to hurt the unicorn, but the act of speaking stabbed her from the inside. Iraem was so, so tall, and the mist so thick. The hissing of the snakes and the sliding of scales as they moved dug into her, made it hard to breathe.

Hold on, Adren.

As if borne by a gentle wind, a memory rose from the dark place in Adren's mind. Trees surrounded her, shafts of light from sun through cedar struck the ground like swords. Like *that* sword.

She was about ten, air scraping in and out of her lungs as if she'd been exerting herself almost to her breaking point. A scream pierced the air as the unicorn—also younger, and by no means fully-grown—wheeled in disjointed circles. It reared, forelegs flailing. Though Adren also wanted to give in to the terror in her, she took a deep breath and stepped towards the unicorn. It screamed again and lashed out at her with its hooves. One connected, drawing blood on her cheek. She stumbled back, hand to her face.

"Please," she said to it in soothing tones. The word came out a little malformed, so she tried again. "Please. I know you're scared, but we can get through this."

The unicorn didn't seem to hear. It drew back from her, body hunched and ears flicking around like mad. Adren began to hum a lullaby. Her voice came out rough at first and she hit more than a few wrong notes, but she eased into it. As the melody smoothed out, she transitioned from humming to wordless song. The unicorn stopped and stared, nostrils quivering. It kept a wary eye on her as she walked to it and hugged its neck, as much to comfort it as to take comfort from the simple warmth of its body.

"Just hold on. You're going to be fine." The lie burned on her tongue.

When Nadin and Loram exited the mound to discover that Adren had gone, Nadin came close to hyperventilating and had to sit down.

"You really don't like your family," Loram commented as she put a hand on his shoulder.

"And you really don't like the fairies in your mound." He took a deep breath. "You seem pretty quick to work against them."

"Fair point. Although it's only a few I hate. Most of the rest are unpleasant enough that it makes the entire situation one I'd much rather get out of."

"Because of your status."

Loram drew back. "That was unkind."

"I'm sorry." Nadin pressed his hands into his forehead. "I have a hard time seeing any other reason why you'd want to leave when Hin asked. Especially when you all here seem more than happy to treat people awfully just to get what you want."

"Some of us want to do better," said Loram quietly. "But our monarchs' rule makes it difficult."

"I can understand that." With a sigh, Nadin stood. "Now. Where do you think Adren is?"

"That depends. Is she the vengeful sort?"

"I— I don't know."

"If she is, she'll go for Iraem, which means she's in the town. If not, perhaps she went to find the monarchs and make a deal with them, in case you failed. Which, now that I think about it, would also mean she would go to the town. And, if she's in trouble, we'll want to bring something with us to help her get out of it."

"Do you have anything like that on your cart?" asked Nadin.

"I like the way you think, part-fae."

They went back into the mound and pulled out the cart.

Although Loram wanted to pull it into town, Nadin talked her out of the idea. If Adren needed help, they needed to be there as soon as they could, and preferably not out of breath. So Loram worked out two enchantments for the cart: one to keep the wheels spinning, another to allow them to turn it when they needed to. After a quick test, they clambered on the cart. Loram stayed in the back to fiddle with the objects in the cart and make them more useful, while Nadin had the honour of making sure they didn't crash into anything too badly.

"I hate enchantments, especially ones you have to cast every time," Loram said. "They're nowhere near as fun as spells."

"Then why do you have a cart full of enchanted objects?"

"It's a business." She shrugged. "And most of them have spells waiting in them anyways."

"What's the difference between enchantments and spells? I always thought they were two words for the same thing." Nadin stuck out his tongue as he kept the cart from wobbling after it hit a bump in the path.

Loram gave him a surprised look, then laughed. "You really don't know? Spells are magic cast on living things. Enchantments are cast on, well, everything else."

"That's it?"

"That's it."

As Nadin grew less clumsy with the steering, they sped up until the wind of their movement rushed past faster than the trees. A few birds scolded them from the undergrowth.

"What about glamour and the Sight? Adren told me no

one uses those words."

"Humans call fairy magic glamour, especially the illusions, and most call a lot of other magic glamour. But anyone who knows anything about how magic is used, humans included, doesn't use that word. It makes you sound ignorant and superstitious."

"Oh." Nadin made a show of inspecting his fingernails, at which Loram laughed again.

"Pay attention to where we're going! The Sight refers to humans with fairy ancestry back far enough they don't remember when, who can see magic like or almost like they can. As well as some other abilities some humans claim they have."

"What kind of abilities?" Nadin frowned.

"No idea. Seeing the future? Knowing things they couldn't possibly know? Things like that, I think. Some humans say it's because one of their ancestors was a saint." She snorted. "As if anyone would believe that. Humans."

Nadin cleared his throat uncomfortably.

"Never fear, I don't mean you." Loram grinned. "You've got fae blood, after all."

After some hesitation, Nadin gave a watery smile.

They raced through the forest, faster than the illusion on the pathway could open up for them, but it tried the best it could, causing the not-forest to flicker around them as they rode through it. When they arrived in town, Nadin glanced back at the pathway just as the illusion snapped back into place, almost as if telling them good riddance.

"Now," Loram muttered, "where is Adren?"

Adren rubbed her forehead, but it didn't make the stinging go away. Only the phrase "hold on" remained of the receding memory. Towering over her, Iraem smiled again, this time with warmth.

"Shall we end this useless talk and return to the mound?"

As the snakes writhed around her, Adren considered her options.

The first: go with Iraem, let the fairy call her pet and plaything until she finally learned how to do good for the unicorn. She could apply herself to that, and these fairies might find a way to help it. Perhaps she could even convince them to help Nadin, rather than capture him as well. And they would remove the last remains of the spell from Adren. This path held all the things she wanted, so did it really matter that she would be called things that rankled her?

Yet she wasn't a child anymore; if she needed teaching, that should be her choice, not theirs. Except Iraem hadn't given an ultimatum. She'd asked a question. So suppose Adren said no and decided to go home to be taught instead, among fairies she knew and who knew her. She could find someone else to remove the spell threads, someone to help Nadin. Nothing for the unicorn.

A flash of steel deep within her refused to let this sway it. She didn't need to learn anything. She had her morality straight and Iraem and the other fairies didn't. This steel couldn't pin down any specifics as to why this might be true. Or none where Iraem's morality gone awry was the only plausible explanation. All it could offer was stubbornness.

The unicorn stamped and shook its mane.

Maybe it really was so terrible to be called a plaything.

"Silence for too long becomes boring," said Iraem. "You should keep that in mind."

"I won't. I'm not going back to the mound with you."

"You should reconsider. I'm offering you an opportunity you won't find again."

Adren snorted. "You'll have to try better than that."

With a collective hiss, the snakes stopped their undulation and poised to strike. Iraem had said it would hurt worse next time, that it would leave marks. Iraem had also said the unicorn wasn't a unicorn. She had likely already decided it couldn't heal.

Adren looked Iraem right in the eyes—not the eyes of her tall illusion-self, but at the place where Adren knew her real eyes would be—and walked through the snakes.

Iraem hadn't lied. Where she passed through the serpentine barrier, Adren's skin felt on fire. She gritted her teeth and forced her way through to the sound of the unicorn screaming as it charged Iraem. If the fairy had had a defense planned, she didn't put it up in time. The unicorn's horn tore right through her illusion, breaking it. The white spear missed Iraem's true body, but the creature behind it did not, and knocked her over.

Like steam, the snakes melted into the air. Adren's pain gone, the unicorn halted. It kept its horn lowered and had turned to prepare itself for another charge. Where or how Iraem lay on the ground, Adren couldn't tell through the mist, so she backed away just in case. The spell in her mangled the coordination of the muscles of one leg and it failed her. Down she went, into the white surround.

The cart clattered through the streets as Loram scanned the town for Adren. They didn't see any fairies in that part of town, but both Nadin and Loram had several magic objects nearby, rigged to release spells without much fuss. Loram hadn't said exactly what all of them would do, but she seemed pleased by the few she held. When Nadin had asked about then, she'd refused to answer. He kept giving her nervous side glances after that until the roads became twisty enough to need his full attention.

"Do you think you could slow this down a bit?" he asked after they almost took the siding off a house. "I really don't have as much experience with this kind of thing as you seem to think."

"Shh," said Loram as she waved at him. "Did you see that?"

"What?"

"Towards the market, I think in it, a spell collapsed. It wasn't far above the mist, but I caught it. Might it be Adren?"

"Might it be?" Nadin snorted. "I'd bet money that's Adren." He turned the cart onto the south-going main road and they headed into the market.

TEN

Before Adren could get back to her feet, someone grabbed her by the ankle and pulled her down.

Iraem.

Adren kicked and the fairy let go with a cry. But when she stood again, Adren found herself surrounded by thick mist. Panic shuddered its way to her from the unicorn. No pain, not yet, but Adren's throat closed as she tried to make her way to where the unicorn had been.

The multi-headed form of a dragon took shape in the mist.

"Really?" Adren said. "Is that the *only* terrifying creature you fairies can think of?"

Its eyes glowed as its ghostlike body charged at Adren, only to dissipate a moment later as if blown by the wind. The sparks from its eyes scattered, forming a ring around Adren. She readied herself for an attack. Around each spark, the mist formed into grotesque shapes: gaping maws, hollow eyes, claws extended and quivering as if they might strike of their own volition if given a chance. The horned heads of these creatures rose above Adren's, higher than Iraem's illusion-self had. Demons, every last one of them. And they were hungry.

"No, you can't step on the stair like that, or else it'll creak," a little girl said in Adren's memory. "Which means you've woken the demon under it and now it's grumpy. And we wouldn't want to know what happens if it's grumpy for too long, now would we?" There came a giggle. "Of course I know demons aren't real, but it makes for a fun game, doesn't it?"

Adren smiled.

The unicorn opted for greater panic, which made Adren grow serious again. If Iraem took proper advantage of the opportunities that came to her, she might trick the unicorn into hurting Adren without Adren knowing what hit her.

Or she would try. So long as Adren kept close enough attention to her sense of the unicorn's location, Iraem wouldn't succeed. Such small changes wouldn't be easy to notice, but if these demon-illusion—

As if they'd heard her think about them, the demons lunged at Adren.

As soon as they arrived in the market, Loram removed the enchantment that kept the cart going. This, of course, wasn't the same as stopping, so Nadin still had to keep it from hitting things as it rolled to a halt. Which it didn't do quickly. When they spotted Adren, Iraem, and the unicorn, and tried to get next to them, the cart opted instead to pass right by with a clatter and plow into the stall behind them instead.

They hadn't disrupted the illusion surrounding Adren, but they *had* almost hit Iraem. She had set an illusion around herself as well to make herself look like Adren, and had been approaching the unicorn. That hadn't been working well. The unicorn kept lashing out at her with its hooves and backing away, ears flat against its head. It seemed for a moment they would run into her, but she must have heard them coming and stepped neatly out of the way.

Shaken by the crash, neither Nadin nor Loram got out of the cart right away. Nadin groaned and, under the pretense of doubling over, checked his pocket to make sure the wooden hand hadn't fallen out. It hadn't. He almost let out a sigh of relief, but caught himself mid-inhale and checked to make sure Loram hadn't heard. By this point, though, Loram had left the cart and headed straight for Iraem, two magical objects in each hand. Grabbing a couple to put into his other pocket, Nadin got up.

Most of the illusion surrounding Adren, being mist, made it impossible to tell if any other magic had also come out to play. That said, the demons and the sparks in their chests were visible, as was Adren. Without even a pause, Nadin ran right into the illusion.

Adren ducked under the demons' attacks, dodged between their legs, and made a general nuisance of herself. The more complicated she made this for Iraem, the harder it would be for the fairy to keep up both this illusion and whatever she might be doing to the unicorn.

Of course, the lingering spell threads made this difficult. She had already sustained a burn on one arm when it had locked up, and a tail had hit her in the stomach when she'd almost tripped over her own feet. None of this prevented her escape. It didn't need to; she couldn't leave. No matter how she tried, she kept finding herself heading back to the circle of demons over and over again.

Her latest attempt ended in her ducking as a demon swung at her, followed by Nadin appearing at her side.

"Hell, hell, hell, hell, hell," he said, shaking his arms as if they'd gone to sleep. "The magic blocking the way in here stings. Also: Hi, Adren." His smile left his face the moment he saw her. "What happened to you?"

Rather than respond, she pointed at the demons, two of which were about to skewer her and Nadin with their claws. Adren and Nadin leapt in opposite directions, and Adren scrambled to get out of the way of the rest of the demon coming her way.

"Magic in an illusion? What for?" muttered Nadin, much to Adren's amusement. "Adren, how can I help?"

"Getting me out of here would be useful. I keep getting turned around."

"Got it. Uh. Could you come to me first?"

The demon which had missed Adren turned to face her again.

"Sure. Just keep talking so I know where you are." He wouldn't have a problem with that.

"Uh. Okay." At which point, he launched into an

extraordinarily detailed monologue about how he'd convinced Loram to help and how the two of them had rigged the cart to get to town faster. Adren couldn't help but chuckle. Who knew verbosity could come in so handy? And, miracle of miracles, he'd hit on a topic Adren found fascinating indeed. She wasn't sure what it meant that Loram had decided to go against Iraem, but she liked what it did for their chances.

"All right, shut up," she said once she'd reached him. He obliged. "Get me out of here."

Her hand on his shoulder, he led her away from the demons. Before the illusion could interfere with her sense of sight, she closed her eyes and listened. The sounds of the demons kept moving, as if she was circling them instead.

What she wouldn't give to be able to close her ears. It really was too bad that Nadin either couldn't or didn't know how to make illusions of his own.

"Careful," he said. "We're about to walk through a barrier. It's going to hurt, but it won't last long."

"Fine with me."

It was worse than the snakes. Adren squeezed Nadin's shoulder hard enough that she was sure she left bruises. But he kept going and she followed until the mist above her shoulders had cleared to its previous state.

Not far from them, Loram and Iraem faced each other next to a burning stall. At least, Adren *thought* it was Iraem. Her appearance had changed, as if she'd shrunk and the colour in her skin and hair had been almost completely leached out. Behind her, the unicorn did a nervous dance, its confusion loud in Adren's mind.

"Do I really look like that?" Adren asked.

"Someone's going to need to put that out," Nadin observed at the same time.

They gave each other a look.

"Haven't you seen yourself in a mirror before?" Nadin asked.

"Not often."

He shrugged.

Loram swung at Iraem, her fist made odd by whatever she held in it. The blow landed on the side of Iraem's head with more force than Adren had thought Loram could muster. Iraem crumpled.

"I would have blocked that," Adren commented. "Or grabbed her arm, sidestepped, thrown her to the ground. That would have been even better." Aside from her own entertainment, saying this kept her calm. If the unicorn believed that Iraem was Adren, and if it believed Adren was in distress, it would try to help. Which meant attacking Loram. Adren wasn't interested in losing any allies.

"Shouldn't we do something?" asked Nadin. "I have these." He pulled out of his pocket some of the items Adren remembered from Loram's cart.

"What do they do?"

"I'm not sure."

Adren sighed. "Then don't use them. We don't want to hurt the unicorn or Loram by accident. Does Iraem look like she's going to get up?"

"Maybe? She's not moving very quickly."

The fact that Loram hadn't moved in to attack Iraem made Adren hesitant. But the fact that the unicorn hadn't yet caught on to her and Nadin's presence meant she would have to act soon.

"I need to get the unicorn out of there," Adren said. "But this idiot spell could act out at any moment, and if Iraem notices me, she'll try to manipulate the unicorn and I don't want to have to deal with that."

"You're doing that thing again. The one where you tell me things. Why are you telling me things?"

Adren glared. "Less questioning. More helping."

"You might find a barrier useful," said Denyeh.

Both Nadin and Adren jumped at her voice. She was crouched behind a stall, scrutinizing Loram.

"Why are you there?"

"There are fairies invading and a commotion in the marketplace. Where else would I be?"

Adren gestured at the entire rest of the town.

"Nadin!" yelled Loram. Iraem, illusion shed, had almost got back to her feet. The unicorn danced back from her, panic rising.

"Me?"

"What do you have in your pockets?"

He pulled out some more items Loram had had on her cart. She nodded, and a purple blast shot from Nadin's hand at Iraem.

"Nadin!" cried Adren.

"It wasn't me!" he said.

Iraem raised a hand. The blast parted, covering the stalls

behind her in sparks. It didn't hit the unicorn, but it had come close, and Adren couldn't seem to quiet the unicorn with her own emotions.

"You may want to know," said Denyeh as Loram lunged at Iraem, "that that fairy just sent a message to the others. They'll be here soon. I can make a barrier that will keep us safe as we get out of here."

"You called the soldiers on us," said Adren. "How do I know you really want to help?" Would it be possible for her to sneak up to the unicorn without being caught up in Loram's and Iraem's fight?

"Did you not hear a word I just said? The other fairies are coming. All of them. The only way you'll be safe from them if they get here before you can leave is with my help."

"She's right, Adren," said Nadin. "None of the fairies could get past her barrier at the prison."

Adren took stock. A panicking unicorn, two angry fairies, Nadin, and herself. And all of them except one fairy needed to escape in the barrier. Even if Denyeh called the soldiers again later, they would be up against a formidable force. Adren liked those odds.

"We'll need everyone here in the barrier except the one that called the other fairies. Can you do that?"

Denyeh looked startled. "I can make one big enough, but I'll have to start it around the fairy or else she won't be able to get in. Then the rest of us will have to get inside."

Adren nodded. Only a little longer, she tried to communicate to the unicorn. Stay put for just a little longer.

Iraem had fallen again, but Loram kept her distance this

time and yelled at her instead. Illusion stopped Adren from being able to hear it so, as Denyeh started her enchantment, Adren leaned over to Nadin.

"What's she saying?" she asked in a low tone.

"She's mad at Iraem for something." He paused. "It's all that funny talk. I'm having a hard time following."

"That 'funny talk' is the dialect of magical creatures. What's she saying?"

"Sorry." Nadin flushed. "Uh…" He scrunched his face together. "Iraem bared Loram's back to someone. Is that a metaphor? Oh. Oh. Adren, Iraem's the reason why the hand was in the prison. She made it so the soldiers caught Loram when it was empty. Because she was jealous of Loram? Something about kidnapping someone. Ugh, and Iraem's just laughing at her."

Adren was going to have to make sure Nadin learned some of the dialect when they got to her home. He couldn't expect to travel with her and get along when he had this hard of a time relaying it back to her. That said, she didn't know whether Iraem baring Loram's back was a metaphor, either. She'd heard it before a few times from the fairies she'd grown up with, but they'd never explained what it meant.

"Kidnapping who?" asked Denyeh.

Nadin frowned. "She's not saying. And I think the barrier's up. Something happened, but I lost it. Loram stopped yelling, at any rate."

"Is it?" Adren asked. Denyeh nodded and followed Nadin to Loram while Adren went to get the unicorn. It spotted her at once and went to her, laying its head over her shoulder as it trembled. She hummed in its ear, alert to any movement on Iraem's part, but there was none. The unicorn walked with her to the others, where Denyeh and Loram stared at each other like two cats having a territorial dispute. Adren rolled her eyes. They didn't have time for this.

"We're leaving. Now," was all she said as she ushered them all away from Iraem. Nadin seemed relieved by this and went at once. Loram and Denyeh resisted, but the stirring of mist where Iraem lay convinced them. As they went, Iraem stood, her cheek dark with what would become an impressive bruise the next day. She could do nothing to stop them from leaving and it only took a glance for Adren to tell that she knew it.

Good.

ELEVEN

The other fairies noticed them all in their barrier soon enough and followed, testing it. Unlike the barrier at the prison, this one didn't let in any of their magic, but that didn't stop them from surrounding it with their illusions. Weird, deformed creatures filled the streets before them, hissing, roaring, swooping down from shifting rooftops. The metal of the streetlamps glowed with sickly colours. Behind them, buildings shimmered like the air on a hot day, while the mist became a white ocean complete with waves and filled with sea creatures of all kinds.

Loram, unimpressed, led the group through these while Adren soothed the unicorn, and they were soon at Denyeh's house. Once they were inside, Denyeh put up a new barrier around her property, and a few fairies remained outside it to lurk.

Inside the house, they settled on the most sensible course of action first: food. And sleep. Nadin and Adren especially needed the latter. Even though it was the middle of the day, the amount they had gone through had drained them both. Denyeh, despite her clear distrust of Loram, made sure they all had what they needed. While Loram removed the rest of the spell from Adren, Nadin helped Denyeh prep the bed he was to sleep in.

"How did you know the fairy had sent a message?" Nadin asked.

"I have the Sight," Denyeh said with a shrug. "Not much, but enough to give me a good intuition about things, especially when magic's involved."

"So it's real?"

Denyeh fluffed a pillow and gave him a funny look. "Of course it's real. Did someone tell you otherwise?"

"Loram said she wasn't convinced it was. Well, not all of it. Only if someone's part fairy and can see magic, I guess."

"That's because fairies think they're the centre of everything," Denyeh said with a snort. "Grab that end of the sheet and pull it over. Yes, like that. Remember what I told you about the saint?"

"The one who lost the gauntlets?"

She nodded. "According to the story, the reason the saint was tricked by the demon was because the water was a source of great power. The demon claimed that the removal of the gauntlets before drinking it would allow some of that power to go to the saint's family and keep them safe from harm."

"Who would want to harm the family of a saint?" The sheet had become twisted and, no matter what he did, Nadin couldn't get it undone.

"The thought never crossed the saint's mind. One who wore gauntlets that give invulnerability only does so because they are afraid of harm, whether real or imagined. So the saint removed them and drank." Denyeh shooed Nadin away from the bed and straightened out the sheet.

"But the water didn't give the saint's family power, did it? The demon had to have been lying."

"That's the funny thing—it wasn't. According to the story, some of that water's power *did* go to the saint's family, who lived here in this town. That's where they say the Sight comes from. It certainly does pop up more in some families than others." Sheet in place, Denyeh threw the pillow to Nadin and picked up a blanket.

"Do you think that's where it comes from?" Nadin fussed with the exact position of the pillow.

"It's as good an explanation as any. The fairies could be right, of course, and it could be that it's from bits of fairy blood still hanging around in the families here. But no one really knows, and it's not as if we know enough about the saints to say for certain one didn't send power down from a pool on the way to heaven. Stop that." Taking the pillow from him, Denyeh stared Nadin down until he backed off and picked up the blanket.

"I suppose."

"Now, see, if *you'd* said you had the Sight, then I'd know it was from your fairy blood."

"You've got it wrong—" He stopped as Denyeh threw the pillow in place and put her hands on her hips.

"Why do you think I called the soldiers on you? I have

a warning signal set up to tell me if there's a fairy in the market, and another for if that fairy is at my stall. I thought for certain that you would use your magic to hide or confuse the soldiers and then escape, but you didn't. So I supposed you must be part human."

"You mean the soldiers didn't think I was a Breimic spy?" Nadin meekly spread the blanket over the bed.

"No, they did. It was the only way they'd listen to me—they don't want to deal with the fairies. Plus, you did start acting strange when I mentioned the planned war with Breim, and the fairies here do sometimes have visitors from Breim. You can hear it in their accents." With crisp, efficient movements, Denyeh straightened out the blanket to her specifications.

"So then why did you—?"

"Later." Denyeh laughed and indicated the bed. "You need to sleep. Thank you for your help and, for what it's worth, I'm sorry I misjudged you. Seeing what you did today, it's clear you're not what I thought you were."

Nadin nodded and she left. He sat on the bed for a while, staring into space, before he lay down, adjusted the pillow, and went to sleep.

As soon as Denyeh and Nadin were out of earshot, Adren began asking Loram all the questions she'd been storing up ever since the whole mess began, starting with:

"What's so important about that saintsall wooden hand?"

"An you wish me to give the secrets of my mound, I shall not say them. Know that before you essay to learn from me.

Also know that your magic changed the spell greatly and removing it such that you are at ease requires much of my attention." To Adren's surprise, although such statements should carry a threat behind them, she found none. Instead she heard only Loram's firm tone and tasted the sweetness of honeysuckle. So she decided to respond in kind.

"I only planned on passing through this town on the way home, and now I've antagonized an entire fairy mound to the point of them mounting an invasion. It's clear that I've both entered and then stirred up the hornet's nest and I need to know how to keep from being stung any more."

Loram sighed. "That wooden hand, called the Demonic Vessel, is an old, old fairy relic. As Nadin likely told you, it may contain magic, and the monarchs give use of it to a fairy as a sign of trust. I had it, and lost it through foolishness when captured and imprisoned by the humans. It was, at the time, depleted of magic, but now that it has magic in it again, we must needs take it back. We know not how it may do what it does, and we fear what humans may do if they learn the secret of it. Thus, all in the mound who the monarchs trusted came to take back what is ours."

"Was Iraem the reason you lost it in the first place?"

A muscle in Adren's leg spasmed as the spell thread which Loram had been removing knotted up inside.

"Nadin told me as much as he could of what you said to her while she lay on the ground."

"Aye, she caused the whole thing. She goaded me into using the magic too quickly and then left me vulnerable."

Encouraged by this, Adren continued with the train of

thought she'd developed on the way to Denyeh's house. "And so, when Nadin convinced you to help him, you agreed because of Iraem, not him?"

Loram gave Adren a funny look. "Aye," she said slowly.

Of course, that left out why Iraem had left Loram in such a situation, but Adren liked how well the explanation fit. Loram and Iraem had had friction in the mound, after all, and Iraem's actions towards Adren made more sense as a fairy who went too far with some of her decisions. Which was still wrong, especially in the way Iraem seemed to have done it, but forgivable. Adren still wasn't about to go learn anything from Iraem, but she could let go of the unpleasantness she'd had in her stomach about their encounters.

The last spell thread quivered as it began to dissolve. It wriggled away from Loram's magic, almost as if it had a life of its own. Adren's magic tried to fling it out, but it slipped to the side, contorting in Adren's mind, near where the full spell had caused Adren's memory to go berserk. She held her breath as it inched closer to that place, hoping that, by doing so, nothing would go wrong.

"Keep still," muttered Loram.

The thread did not keep still. But it did disappear, even if after flicking that part of Adren's mind. Along with her sigh of relief, she gave a prayer of thanks.

"That was an unpleasant spell."

"It was only meant to keep you still while letting you think you still ran. How it broke apart like this, I cannot say, but from its shape it seems your magic made it something it was not. Unpleasant as it was meant to be, whatever you experienced was not its intended effect." Loram frowned. "If I knew how to place your magic, I would be able to say more."

"You don't recognize it?"

"I cannot recognize it. There is something broken in it, and so its true nature is hidden from me. It bothers me, and has since I first saw you. Do you not know what it is?"

"No. I know not, though I dearly wish I did."

"What of the unicorn?"

Iraem's reaction to the unicorn flooded Adren's mind. "What of it?"

"The magic in it is also... broken. I would use another word, but I cannot think of one to describe what I see."

Adren shivered. She wanted to talk to Loram about it, Loram who could see and who would know what might be the cure for the unicorn's condition. And yet, the hair on the back of her neck rose with just the thought of telling Loram that the unicorn was insane. A knot formed in her throat and she wanted to reach out to the unicorn for comfort, but it had nodded off and its emotions had become fuzzy.

"Iraem didn't believe it was a unicorn when she saw it."

"An I had not seen it heal, I would still believe the same. And yet I doubt."

"Why?"

Loram sighed. "Adren, may I be frank with you? It is clear you care about the unicorn, so I will speak no more on this an you wish it."

A chill curled under Adren's ribcage. "What's wrong?"

"I do not know an the unicorn's magic is such because

another has twisted it or an it has always had this affliction. Either way, I fear what might happen should someone try to make that magic whole. It may be a unicorn and nothing more, but it may also cast that off as a disguise to reveal something... horrible. I know not what. The cure you seek is for the unicorn, is it not?"

Eyes hot with unshed tears, Adren kept silent. She couldn't be hearing this. It couldn't be true.

"Please, Adren, I beg you: do not try to heal it. It is better that it stays as it is."

Sweetness spread over Adren's tongue. No, no, no! She tried to fight it down, attribute it to something innocuous. But her truth sense would not be denied. Loram believed her plea with all her heart. She stood.

"I need to rest," she told Loram. "Thank you for removing the spell."

And she fled the room, fighting herself all the way. Denyeh, who she met on the way, started to say something but, with one look at Adren's face, stopped and let her by. Heat rose in Adren's cheeks as she imagined what Denyeh might have seen. Gods in hell, next Nadin would come in and ask her what was wrong. This was why Adren preferred to solve problems on her own; people, human or not, were too saintsall nosy for their own good. Too willing to give advice she didn't want or need. As she lay back on the bed, she tried to distance herself from what was happening inside. It took a long time before she was finally able to sleep.

A man sat by the fire and, though she knew he wasn't blind, Adren wondered if he could see her. As she watched him, the fire melted away and it might have been the same man who now stood before her. His clothes were no longer black, which could have been enough except he reminded her of the first man. The face would have told her, but she could not see his face, just as she had not seen a face by the fire.

Regardless, this standing man held a sword in one hand. He raised it, and though she could not see his face, she knew it was contorted in rage. Adren leapt forward to stop him, only for him to swing the sword down at her and for the burning pain in her forehead to start all over again. She stared at him, her whole body shaking, her thoughts disjointed. No matter how long she tried, she couldn't put together the pieces. It was as if she brought them together only for them to push each other away the moment they touched. But it was all she had, and so she kept trying to bring them together and they refused to fit over and over again.

Her forehead ached. Adren noticed this in a decreasingly detached way. It ached more than she had thought it ever could. Her disbelief at the whole situation, her scrambling to understand, only grew as that ache continued. And, beneath it, growing even faster, was an emotion she had never felt before and which terrified her. Its rising accelerated with each breath she took, pulling everything in her into its gaping jaws. A tightness had begun in her chest; a knot formed in her stomach. She couldn't speak. She couldn't think. She couldn't believe.

Who had done this to her?

And why?

Icy fingers curled around her heart, spread outward through her veins. Breathing had become difficult. Who could have done this?

Had it been her fault?

No, it couldn't have been, her rational mind countered. She had done nothing to provoke such violence. There was obviously something wrong with this man.

But he was yelling and the words... she couldn't remember the words, but they shrank her nonetheless. Lies, every last one, the kind of lies that flew like arrows into the heart until you could do nothing but curl up and become so, so small. These words broke the power of her mind. The rising flood beneath it broke through to freeze her blood and burn her heart.

I am...

I am...

Someone was shaking her. She opened her eyes. An unfamiliar room. A familiar face.

"Adren!"

Nadin didn't wake slowly—open bleary eyes, stare around a bit, yawn, take your time sitting up. That kind of waking is reserved for those who have had enough sleep and are ready to continue the day, and Nadin had slept nowhere near enough for that. He woke because of the screaming.

Stumbling out of bed, thwacking his arm on the doorframe, he rushed into the room Adren was sleeping in. There she lay, face screwed up and skin covered in sweat as she screamed at the top of her lungs. Denyeh and Loram ran in behind him.

"I thought you got rid of the spell!" Denyeh said as she reached for Adren, only to be pushed aside by her thrashing.

"Aye, I did! The spell has not caused this."

"Then what has?"

Nadin ignored them. "Not again," he said, face pale. Kneeling by the bed, he took Adren by the shoulders and shook. Her eyes opened, but they were unfocused. "Adren!"

"Nadin?" Clear now, she glanced down at Nadin's hands. "You can let go now, you know. Nadin. I'm fine. It was just a dream."

"No, you're not fine. It was the man with the sword again, wasn't it?"

"It'll go away in time. It always does. Now let go."

"Adren, I'm not going to let go. You need help."

"No, no!" Adren pulled herself from Nadin's grasp. "I don't need help here. When I get home. That's when I get help."

At this, Nadin gave the other two a pleading look.

Loram backed away. "I have no aid I may offer." She slipped out of the room.

With a roll of her eyes at both Loram and Nadin, Denyeh addressed Adren. "How long has this been happening?"

"I'll be fine."

"Nadin just ran in here, woken from a dead sleep from you screaming, said 'not again' and woke you up without another thought. That tells me it's been going on for far too long."

Adren glared.

"It's been three weeks," Nadin offered.

"No, I want to hear it from Adren." After Adren had remained silent enough for it to be awkward, Denyeh continued. "You may think you don't need to be well to deal with this gods-damned mess you and Nadin blundered through when you arrived here, but if you continue this way, you won't only hurt yourself. You'll get him hurt, the unicorn, and everyone in this town. If this was only your problem, I would let you go, send you on your merry way until you either destroyed yourself with your foolishness or woke up to what you're doing to yourself and changed how you dealt with this. But this isn't just you. This is me. This is my town, the people that I care about, and I will not let your selfishness give the fairies an opening or a reason to destroy what I love any more than they already have. Have I made myself perfectly clear?"

Nadin cleared his throat. "I'll... be with Loram. If you need me." Before either of them could answer, he escaped to the main room.

Yelling erupted behind him, followed by a slammed door. The main room was empty, but he found Loram when he wandered into the yard. She sat, watching the unicorn try to unlatch the gate.

"It won't get out, will it?" asked Nadin.

"I put an enchantment on the latch to keep it closed," said Loram. "It won't be getting out."

"Oh. Good." Nadin sat down next to her.

Together they watched the unicorn in silence as it stopped

nibbling at the gate latch and stuck its horn under it instead.

"I wonder how it tasted," Nadin commented.

Loram shrugged.

The unicorn wiggled its horn under the latch for a bit.

"Probably like metal," Loram said.

It was back to nibbling again. The unicorn got a firm grip on the latch with its mouth and pulled it up. That done, it nosed open the gate. Nadin stood.

"I thought you said it couldn't move it."

"Well, it did now!"

"Should we go after it?" They watched as, gate open, the unicorn trotted out of the yard.

"That might be a good idea."

The two of them went after the unicorn but, as it had gone past the barrier, only Nadin could follow.

"Tell Adren the unicorn got out!" he yelled back at Loram, who nodded and went back into the house. Nadin, on the other hand, had to run to catch up with the unicorn, who was going at a good pace by now.

"Why am I always running everywhere?" he complained.

He followed the unicorn to the forest. Unlike its usual wanderings, this time it headed in a straight path, as if it had a destination in mind, somewhere northwest. They crossed the main road, Nadin checking it despite the fact that it was empty. Some distance west of the fairy mound, the unicorn turned, its movement still purposeful, and headed northeast. It slowed, too, and Nadin was able to walk most of the time, with the occasional jog when he fell behind.

They continued this way for a bit longer until it was as

if the unicorn had hit a wall. It backed up, tossing its head. Then it lowered its horn and charged, only to be thrown to the side. With a snort, it got up and tried again, to the same result. Before it could try a third time, Nadin put a hand on its shoulder. It flinched and pulled away.

"Let me try," he said.

The simple fact was that the unicorn had come up against a barrier. Its origin point wasn't clear, but the magic that made it had come from fairies. Nadin went up to the barrier and held out a hand. It slid through the barrier with ease. The same thing happened when he tried to walk through.

"Must be meant just to keep non-fairies out." He chuckled. And stopped, eyes wide and shoulders turned as if he was about to run.

Magic rushed towards him. Not fairy magic. The kind of magic that had been in the fake hand. He backed out of the barrier, but it was only meant to keep humans out. The bright river poured its way towards Nadin. He squeezed his eyes shut.

TWELVE

"I don't care about your town," said Adren. "And I'll get help as soon as I'm back home. Which will be soon. I have this under control." Denyeh's accusations of foolishness and selfishness burned in Adren's heart.

"Really? It doesn't look that way to me."

"That's because you haven't seen much to begin with."

"Adren." Denyeh sat on the end of the bed. Adren pulled her feet close to her, knowing she was acting like a child, hating every moment of this intrusion on her privacy. "Adren, I don't need to see everything to know that you're hurting. Let me help. Healing is my trade."

"Says the woman who runs a market stall and puts up barriers for prisons."

"The market stall is where I sell produce from my cousin's farm. As for the barriers, I'm the only one in the town who does magic, and they'd caught a fairy." She shrugged. "It was a necessity."

"Loram." After Iraem had made her vulnerable somehow.

"Yes"

"So that's it?" Adren sneered. "You humans see a fairy and think, 'Yes, let's capture it and lock it up'? You have no conscience."

"What about when we see it breaking into our yard, with the White Changeling and a unicorn following along with it?"

Saints. Adren had thought the rumours of her had only spread out in certain circles. "Nadin's not a fairy."

"But you don't deny that you're the White Changeling?"

There wasn't anything to deny. And, it seemed, there wasn't anything to say. Nothing came to mind, at any rate. If it weren't for the fairies outside the barrier, Adren would have made a run for it.

"If I tell you why they locked up Loram, would that help you trust me?"

"That depends on what you say." Or course, Denyeh might lie. She could get through her whole sad story and Adren wouldn't sense a whit of truth from her. Supposing that happened (she *hoped* that happened), how would she and the unicorn get away from Denyeh? Nadin, she could shout at. Loram could get the barrier down, or trap Denyeh in an illusion. But they would still have to leave somehow and get the hand to the fairies or else Adren would never get back home.

"The fairies sometimes sell enchantments and spells in the market. Some are silly, some are useful. Several are a necessity for treating certain illnesses. There are people here with sicknesses none of us can cure, but they can continue to live comfortably because of the spells the fairies sell. Or, at least, they could until the fairies thought it would be entertaining to raise their prices beyond what most could afford. They freely admitted to doing this, too. I couldn't stand it, and learned everything I could about those spells so I could recreate them. My versions weren't quite as good as the fairies' ones, but people could afford them. And the fairies got angry."

"Fairies aren't like that!" Adren cried when she couldn't stand it anymore, swallowing down the honeysuckle. "Magical creatures aren't like that. The only kind of being that does anything like that is the human one."

"We're not the only kind of being that does that," Denyeh said softly. "When the soldiers came and started posting announcements about the draft, my husband took the morning off from managing the prison to help them and never returned. We don't know what the fairies did with him after they took him, but the soldiers who witnessed his capture recognized Loram when she came by the town later, and they returned the favour."

No matter how much she tried, Adren couldn't get rid of the sweetness in her mouth. She swallowed, over and over. She wanted to get a knife and scrape it all out.

"Listen, Adren: you need help. And if you don't get it soon, you'll go face the fairies again and this will happen and you might not make it out. Think whatever you want of me, but you know I'm right."

Saints. Saints, saints, saints. Adren took a deep, shuddering breath. And another. And another. Concern through the connection. Breathe. Breathe. Speak.

"I don't think you *can* help me."

"Do you think anyone here can help you?"

"The fairies, but"—Adren grimaced—"they don't seem to be inclined to do that." Not in the way she wanted, that is.

"If I can't heal this, is there anything else I can do for you?"

Smash down the boundary of the dark place in Adren's mind, perhaps? The potion maker in Watorej had almost managed that by accident. Except Adren wasn't sure she wanted that. Whatever else that place hid, she was sure it would overwhelm her. If Denyeh could stuff everything back inside and repair the crack the potion maker's spell had left, Adren would accept that in a moment.

Even if she lost her magic? It crowded against her skin, all light and heat. Broken, Loram had said. But Loram had also taught her how to use it a little, so it couldn't be too terrible.

"I don't trust you, Denyeh. I don't want to believe you. But I also didn't come here to cause problems. I only want peace." She'd thought she would find it once she found the cure for the unicorn. She'd thought she had it with magical creatures. And now, the fairies had tried to kidnap her and Loram had told her never to heal the unicorn. So what was she supposed to do? The only person in all of this who'd acted decently was Nadin. Possibly also Denyeh, but Nadin for sure.

How could everything have gotten so backwards in less than two days?

Adren almost didn't notice that the unicorn was leaving

through all this, but the way its location changed was unusual enough to call attention to itself. Direct, purposeful movement happened before it got hurt. But the hurt never lasted long. It would run back to Adren, and she would treat any wounds it had except for the one she wanted most to heal.

"What do I do?" Adren asked.

"You choose," said Denyeh. "You choose the life you want to live instead. It's the most powerful magic we have."

Loram opened the door.

"Saints' names!" cried Denyeh. "Don't fairies know how to knock?"

"Can't humans tell when something's important?" Loram retorted. To Adren: "The unicorn escaped. Nadin pursues it for its safety."

"He didn't need to do that. The unicorn will be fine."

"Did the fairies outside follow them?" asked Denyeh.

"Oh no."

"What?" said Adren.

"Neither of us thought to look."

Saints and all the gods besides, Nadin had done it this time.

Nothing in particular had happened to Nadin while his eyes were shut, so he opened them. Only a hand's span away, the magic funnelled down into his jacket pocket, where it was filling the fake hand. The massive stream burned bright enough that, even though only those with the right eyes could see it, the forest around it seemed thrown into shadow.

"Whoa," he breathed. But his awe stopped the moment the unicorn reared and ran off. "Oh no," Nadin said, his expression changing to horror. "What if the fairies...?"

Without another word, he turned and ran. The connection between wherever the river of magic had come from and the wooden hand broke almost at once as he fled. At first, he tried to follow the unicorn, but it headed away from the town so fast that Nadin couldn't keep up. He took a moment to stop and pant for a bit, then turned back and cut across town to Denyeh's house. Inside, everyone had gathered in the main room.

"Where's the unicorn?" asked Loram, but her eyes were on Nadin's pocket.

"Not here, obviously," said Adren, taking a piece of paper from Denyeh and putting it into her own pocket.

"We might have something bigger to worry about," said Nadin. He pulled out the fake hand. "I accidentally filled it partway with magic, and I'm very sure the fairies noticed, so they'll probably be here soon."

"You had that on you the whole time?" Loram peered at Nadin. "What did you do with the magic after you took it from me?"

"He emptied it on me to try and get rid of the spell," said Adren.

"Well, I accidentally made it leak and then tried to stop it. But it worked?" He rubbed the back of his head.

"Mostly," confirmed Adren.

"You seem to do a lot of things by accident," Loram noted. Nadin shrugged.

"How did you fill it with magic, exactly?" asked Denyeh.

"Does it matter? We're going to be surrounded by fairies soon! And the unicorn's still out there somewhere, and we have this hand thing, and Adren's still getting those attacks—unless you fixed that—and... and..."

"Breathe, Nadin," Adren advised as Denyeh directed him to a cushion. He missed the cushion and sat on the floor instead, but he did breathe.

"I never want to run again," he said. The women laughed.

Adren pressed a fist to her chin. The fairies would be stupid not to be coming after Nadin and that hand full of magic. He'd filled it after chasing after the unicorn. How did...? Irrelevant. If the fairies got their Demonic Vessel, they would go back to their mound. Adren, Nadin, and the unicorn could leave without further issues. Loram? Yes, Loram would be the one to give the hand back. They would give her status in return, and all would be well.

What about Denyeh? Her husband? The fairies still had him, and if she was to be believed, the fairies would only continue to harm the people here after they got the hand back.

The hand. The Demonic Vessel. The Saint's Gauntlet. It wasn't a gauntlet, exactly, but neither was it demonic. It may have always belonged to the fairies, too. The saints had forbidden any records made of their lives, after all, and a story told in one small town over who knows how many generations didn't history make. Still, these people had taken the idea of the Saint's Gauntlet from something, and that something must have been the wooden hand.

Adren could find a way to give the hand to the humans instead, let Denyeh use it to help her town. That might not end well for Loram, but she could always come with Adren and Nadin to Adren's home. The fairies there would welcome her, Adren was sure of it.

The only problem with that plan was the soldiers. They knew about the possibility of the Saint's Gauntlet, and they would want it for their war. Denyeh might not be able to keep it from them if someone high enough up heard about it. Adren may not have been in Breim for as long as she could remember, but she still didn't like the idea of bringing it trouble.

"Do you bathe in milk to get your skin that colour?" the girl with the beautiful hair had asked not long after giving Adren her nickname. "Is that something they do in Breim?"

"No! That's just how it is." The accent she'd already been trying to get rid of because of the fairy children's teasing coloured her words even more than usual.

With a firm shake of the head, Adren brought her thoughts back into order. Giving the hand to the humans wouldn't do them much good. They didn't know how to fill it. Plus, the fairies wouldn't leave it with them for long. Even if the humans retaliated...

Adren had an idea. It wasn't much, and she still didn't know what to do about the hand, but she had an idea. At last. Just in time for someone to knock on the door. Denyeh opened it to reveal a group of soldiers.

One of the soldiers spotted Nadin and pointed him out to the others. Nadin shrank back against the wall.

"Why are you here?" Denyeh crossed her arms. "I didn't ask for you to come."

"We're here to make an arrest of the young man who should be in a cell, but who we have discovered was found running through town today," said the one whose insignia indicated he was a captain.

The shortest of the soldiers addressed Nadin. "You'll be happy to know that your cell no longer has an unsanitary wooden hand in it." The others chuckled.

"It would have been unsanitary if it had been real," Nadin muttered, cheeks red.

"Wait." Adren went right up to the captain. Denyeh stepped aside, giving the captain a surreptitious smirk. Even though Adren stood almost a head shorter than him, she more than made up for it with her demeanor. "On what grounds are you arresting him?"

"On the grounds that he's a Breimic spy."

"A... spy. Have you met him? He's..." Rather than come up with a descriptor, she indicated Nadin with one hand. The soldiers around the captain laughed as Nadin slumped. "Besides, what information could he possibly have found? You threw him into prison the moment he got here, and I haven't seen any of you doing anything particularly interesting except arrest him and dodge fairies the whole time we've been here."

"I'm sorry, who are you?" the captain asked.

"The White Changeling. If anyone should be going to

prison here, it's me. But I'm not, and he's not either."

"And why is that?"

"Because you have silly little swords and we have the Saint's Gauntlet."

At this, Nadin stood up. "We do?"

"We heard that once before; we're not falling for it again," said the captain.

Adren rolled her eyes. "Fine. Don't believe me. Arrest Nadin and be done with it. But don't blame me when every single fairy in the mound comes to tear the prison down for it."

"Adren, are you talking about what I think you're talking about?" Nadin's voice strained against his higher register and cracked a few times through his question.

"I'm talking about the unsanitary wooden hand in your coat pocket. Am I right, Loram?"

Adren prayed that, even if she was wrong, Loram would say yes anyways. When she nodded, Adren wanted to cheer.

"Show it to me," the captain said to Nadin, who obeyed. "How do I know you're telling the truth?"

Loram beat Adren to responding.

"Punch him and find out."

What?

"What?" Nadin sounded like he was being strangled.

The captain thought about this a moment and nodded. He punched Nadin in the chest. Nadin fell back, exclaiming loudly.

"That should have cracked a rib," commented the captain.

"Too bad it doesn't protect against pain."

Well, then. Adren hadn't expected that.

"Someone owes me something nice after this," Nadin muttered.

"So you have the Saint's Gauntlet. What do you want?" asked the captain.

"I want you and as many soldiers—as many people, period—as you can find to work with Denyeh, setting up as many barriers around the town as you can before the fairies come up with a plan and move in to get the hand."

"And then what? Sit and twiddle our thumbs for who knows how long while the fairies cut off travel and we die of starvation?"

"You'll sit and twiddle your thumbs, yes. Meanwhile Loram"—she indicated the fairy—"will go to the fairies and tell them I'm going to make a deal with them, which will keep them from attacking. You should let her through now."

"If we don't?"

"Loram?"

The fairy grinned and cast an illusion for the soldiers. They parted, staring at things that didn't exist, and Denyeh opened up enough of the barrier long enough for Loram to duck through and hurry down the street. The soldiers blinked and focused on what was again.

"And now, Captain, you'll help Denyeh with the barriers while Nadin and I head off on our errand."

The captain gave a dry laugh. "What, I have no choice in the matter?"

"Not if you want to protect the people here. Or did I

mistake your occupation for something else?"

"Fine. We'll help her."

Adren nodded at Denyeh, who picked up a bag and headed out with the soldiers.

"Are you going to tell me things again?" asked Nadin, hand back in his pocket, as he rubbed his chest. "Because I know I'm missing something here."

"No, I'm not. We have to find the unicorn first, and you're coming with me."

"Just when I got my hopes up." But he grinned when he said it.

Adren reached into her pocket. Before Nadin had returned, she, Loram, and Denyeh had worked out how to help him if the fairies went after him and the unicorn. Denyeh had grabbed three spoons from her kitchen and, with Loram's help, enchanted them so they could put up a barrier large enough for everyone, including Nadin and the unicorn, to fit. Since this enchantment differed from the fairy barriers, Denyeh instructed both Loram and Adren in the use of it. Loram and Denyeh each carried one with them now, and Adren had hers in her pocket. She activated it the moment she and Nadin left the house.

As they went, Adren shoved a piece of paper at Nadin with a note written on it in crisp handwriting. He opened his mouth.

"It's a list of what we need to get," said Adren. "It'll make sense when you read it."

Although hesitant, Nadin smoothed out the paper and

read the note.

Before you ask, Denyeh wrote this for me, so I hope to all the saints she got it right. Remember the fairies watching the house? Loram says there's only two left after you ran off after the unicorn. If all went well, one is following her and the other is following Denyeh, but we need to be sure. Look behind us, point somewhere (I don't care where) and say, "Shouldn't we go back that way first?" while you check to see if there's a fairy anywhere nearby.

No matter what I say, if you see a fairy, respond with, "I guess I misread that." If there isn't a fairy, say, "This is more complicated than I thought." Act normal.

Nadin followed the instructions to the letter. Stopping all forward motion entirely, he turned back and held his arm fully-extended to point.

"Shouldn't we go to the shop back that way first?" he quavered.

"No," Adren replied, eyebrow raised. "We go there last."

With words so stilted they could have joined a parade on Saints Day, Nadin said "This is more complicated than I thought."

Adren gave a funny sort of cough and resumed walking.

"I was right," she said. "You would make a terrible spy."

"What's that supposed to mean?" said Nadin as he caught up.

"You were even more awkward than usual. If there *had* been a fairy watching us, they would have known we knew." Nadin's face fell, at which Adren snorted. The snort was a bit strained, considering that her sides were still shaking. She cleared her throat. "We would have jumped it if need be. We have options."

"Wait." He pulled out the paper again. "How did you know this was going to happen?"

"I didn't. We'd made that for when we thought we'd have to get you and the unicorn. Now, tell me everything you've seen and heard since we got here, except what you already told me about Loram. I want to be sure I haven't missed anything important."

The story went on even after they'd left town and entered the forest. Adren listened, intent on every word as she led them south to the clearing where she'd left her things. No camp. No sign anyone had come through. Adren rummaged through some bushes until she pulled out her pack. After a quick search, she put it back, hiding it once more. Nadin stared, but didn't comment. He had just gotten to the part when he and the unicorn had arrived at the barrier.

"Wait." Adren held up a hand. "Say that again."

"There was a barrier?"

"No. The unicorn had gone to it. Directly to it. Like it was trying to get to something on the other side."

Nadin's eyes went wide. "Do you think...?"

"I need to see what's on the other side of that barrier."

"Need?" This was accompanied by a gulp.

"Can you take me there?"

"I might be able to..." He rubbed the back of his neck. "Aren't we going to find the unicorn?"

"Yes. On the way." Adren raised an eyebrow.

"What if I can't remember the way?"

She sighed. "Get close to it and look for the magic."

"I-I don't know if I'll be able to see it."

"Nonsense. It's big." She glanced at the bush which hid her pack and adjusted a bit of it with her foot. "Even if you have a hard time seeing part of it, you'll be able to see enough of it to figure out where it is."

"Adren, you don't understand. I really don't know—"

"Remember what you told me about everything you've been doing here?" Bush now behaving properly, Adren fixed her gaze back on Nadin. He looked in every direction but hers.

"Yeah..."

"Why is it that it hasn't been a problem for you to see magic here until right now?"

"I guess... all those other times... I just had to. I never really noticed I wasn't having problems. I just saw it."

"And now?"

Nadin shrugged.

"Well, whatever it is, get over it. It's obvious to me that your ability doesn't come and go like you thought."

"Get over it?" he scoffed. "Like you got over that memory with the man and the sword?"

"Excuse me?" Adren stepped back like she'd been punched. At first, Nadin made as if to placate her, but then he steeled himself and stood tall.

"You don't just 'get over' things, Adren. Not like you seem to think. I mean, look at me. You act like I can do all these things, sure, but then your explanation for why I couldn't be a spy was to just point at me. Is that all I am? A portable magic spyglass that can do or break spells from time to time, but otherwise I'm worthless?"

"I never said you were worthless." The way she looked at him, body half turned, was the way a cat regarded an animal showing bizarre behaviour as it decided whether that animal was dangerous.

"You traded me away to the fairies."

A hawk's cry pierced the stillness between them, cutting it in two. After a bit, the chattering of squirrels broke it again and the trees above rustled as one chased the other out of its territory. Robins warbled as if commenting on the event.

"I trusted you, Adren," Nadin said. "All that time in the prison, I waited for you, worried about you. And you traded me away like I was nothing."

"I thought you might be human."

"That's not right, Adren! I could deal with all the other things—the snide comments, the put-downs, every time you talked over me. But that? How am I supposed to deal with that?" His face reddened as the intensity in his words rose.

"What do you expect me to do?"

"Look at me!"

She put her hands on her hips. "I *am* looking at you."

"No, not just like that." Nadin made as if to tear his hair out. "Look at me. See me. Look at how I've treated you since we first met and tell me that I've earned at least a little of your respect."

THIRTEEN

Depending how you considered it, Nadin had either picked the worst or best time to argue about this. The worst, if you took into account the fact that they had angry fairies waiting on them. The best, if you also took into account that he and Adren were going to walk into the mound with those fairies together.

For all the ways she put Nadin down, Adren had to admit that she was glad she'd agreed to let him travel with her. If he wanted to find out what kind of person he was about to go into danger with, she wanted to know, too.

"Why do you stay with me?"

"What?"

"I can understand why you stuck with me in Watorej—it was exciting, you were helping people, and you barely knew me. But we've been in close quarters for three weeks, and you're right. Yesterday, I traded you off. You could have left me after that. Instead, you got me out, went back to find a way to break the spell on me, bargained with Loram, and got me out of Iraem's illusion. And you're still here. Why?"

"Why did you bring the unicorn in to try to heal my mother?"

Adren squirmed. That had been a test to see if Nadin had been telling the truth about his mother's illness. She hadn't told him that part.

"You're always so careful with the unicorn. We stay off roads for it, we keep it out of cities, we hide it from others. When it's scared, you calm it down. When it's hurt, you treat it. So I've been thinking... why would you risk bringing it into town, into my house where it couldn't run away if it needed to? Why would you bring the thing you cared about the most into danger to help someone who could have been a human in the way you're most scared of?"

She hadn't thought of it that way before. Why *had* she brought the unicorn with her? All she'd needed was herself to confirm what he'd said. Bringing the unicorn back to the forest had almost been a disaster, too. If it hadn't run when it did...

"It was the right thing to do," she finally said, staring at her feet as the meaning of it sank in. She shouldn't have done it; it had been stupid. Just like Nadin shouldn't have rescued her from the mound. He'd said as much afterwards. "Loram told me to stop looking for the cure for the unicorn." She said it slowly, haltingly.

"What? When?" He sounded angry.

"She said its magic is broken in such a way that she's afraid what it might become if someone fixed it. Is that what you see, too?"

"I don't know what a unicorn's magic is supposed to look like, so I never really paid attention. But..." His voice trembled. "Now I really want to pay attention, just to prove that fairy wrong. Come on, let's find that barrier." He started out. Paused. Turned back. "Thank you for telling me that. You didn't have to, you know."

Adren shrugged. Reconsidered her plan of leaving her pack behind and pulled it out. "Let's go." She didn't know how else to respond. After what Loram had said, she'd tried not to think about it, but she'd had this... this feeling. That he'd seen the same thing Loram and Iraem did, and that he'd thought the same. That he'd been laughing behind her back this whole time.

A cool breeze shook the trees as they walked, and a rain of needles fell. In the winter, the bushes and small deciduous trees would lose their leaves, but the pine and cedar would remain green. Even still, though they didn't renew with the seasons, conifers did not remain stagnant. Evergreen, some called them, as if they never changed. They did, but it was a regular discipline. Aspens lost their leaves once in the fall so they could hold tight to them all through the summer. Pine accepted loss as a way of life, and so winter could never make it bare.

Nadin had mentioned snide comments, said she put him down. Talked over him. She couldn't have been doing that with him. Could she? She thought back through all her encounters with him, right from the first time they'd seen each other.

There it all was. Not every time they spoke. Not in

everything she said. But, in her mind, there was so often this idea that she needed to make him better. That he wasn't good enough as he was and that he would never be able to change that, so she had to do it.

Well, he wasn't good enough as he was.

What *was* good enough? By what standard did she judge him?

By the same standard she judged everyone else: herself. As if she was perfect.

No, she knew she wasn't perfect. She knew she didn't reach the standard, either. So what? What was good enough? Was anyone good enough?

Magical creatures had always filled that place, but here she faced fairies who had done wrong. They could be the only ones. Denyeh could have misunderstood what they'd done. Perhaps, knowing what they knew, Aden would find that the fairies had misjudged the actions of Denyeh and the other humans and had acted accordingly.

Still. Nadin, who was mostly if not all human, had never done her wrong. He had his weaknesses, but he had never done anything like on the scale the fairies had.

Even with all his weaknesses, Nadin wasn't the unicorn. The unicorn needed Adren for a cure to the problem it didn't know it had. Nadin, on the other hand, had awareness. He had choice. 'The most powerful magic we have,' Denyeh had said.

Why did that saintsall woman have to be so right?

They found the unicorn first, as Adren had thought they would. She considered it for a moment, while Nadin tried to see if he could figure out what it was about the creature that scared Loram so much. Based on all the head-scratching, he didn't seem to be finding anything. Adren had better luck. With what Iraem had chosen to terrify Adren with after the dragon and what Nadin had told her he'd seen on the walls of the fairy throne room, Adren had a thought of a way to give the monarchs cause to respect or fear her.

"Nadin, give me the hand."

He did. "Why?" She put it in the pocket with the enchanted spoon.

"And take my pack."

Again, he did. "Still waiting on the why."

"When we go to see the monarchs, I'm going to be the one in charge. People in charge don't carry their own things."

"Could we have a plan sometime where I'm the one in charge?"

"I'll keep that in mind."

As she and the unicorn followed him to the barrier, Adren couldn't help but notice how the unicorn's horn seemed to glow in the forest's dappled shade. Like a raised sword.

A sword.

There was something she'd forgotten to tell Nadin.

"I remember everything from the last time the memory attacked me."

"You mean..."

Adren nodded.

"Wow! That's amazing!" He peered at Adren. "That's amazing, right?"

"I don't know what the man's face looks like, or where any

of that happened. It was when I was young, but I don't know how young. So it's not particularly helpful. But I remember a fire, that the man swung his sword at me, and that the unicorn and I ran." The undergrowth thickened, providing Adren an opportunity to focus on it and not Nadin.

"Was the man human?"

"I think so."

"Well, that explains a lot."

Silence. Albeit the kind full of the snap of twigs and rustle of bushes. The caw of crows. The chattering of squirrels. The nervous snort of the unicorn. "Like what?"

"Like you being so..." he ducked under a low-hanging branch, "set on hating humans."

"I didn't always hate humans."

"Well, you sure seem to like doing it for someone who hasn't been doing it long." He was matter-of-fact about it, rather than bitter, like she'd expected. A thought occurred to her.

"Do you think I put you down because you're human?"

"Why else would you do it? You've made it clear to me how terrible you think we are."

"But you're not human." The unicorn paused to nibble on a bush. Adren nudged it back on course.

"Yes, I am."

"Nadin, seriously. You're part fairy. How else could you get through that barrier?"

He scowled. "I guess it's obvious now. Yeah, I've got fairy magic and blood, but I'm not really a fairy. Not like you are, being raised by them. Really, you're more a fairy than

I've ever been."

Adren hadn't thought about it that way. If Nadin was more human than fairy, though, shouldn't it have shown? Like a dog raised by cats. People only make decisions they know how to make, that they know they *can* make. "Isn't your mother part fairy?"

"No. She's completely human."

They also make the decisions they want to make. But where does that desire come from? Is it innate? Or was there something else involved, something Adren couldn't see?

She walked next to the unicorn, hand on its shoulder both for the reassurance of its presence and to keep it at ease so it would stay with her. The two of them had run from the man with the sword. Was that man the same as the one by the fire? Because, if he was, he had betrayed her trust, possibly beyond repair. But if he wasn't, then who was he? She had another memory of the one by the fire crying—he wore the same black clothes in that one—but she didn't know when that had happened. It might have been before. It didn't make sense for it to have been anything but before. The question was how long before and, if he was the same man as the one with the sword, did that mean the two memories connected? Adren had the uncanny feeling they were.

Nadin saw the barrier a long way off. It really was massive, encircling a portion of the forest almost the size of the aboveground area of the mound. When he stood in front of it again, it dwarfed him with ease as it rose in a delicate curve above the forest.

"Can't we just walk through it together?" he asked Adren. "Our barrier doesn't let in fairy magic."

"And the fairy barrier will push back to keep the magic we're using out."

"Why? If it's only keeping people out..."

"With Denyeh making barriers of her own in the town? It'd be silly of them not to protect against magic. Watch." Adren walked to the barrier. The moment the surface of hers met it, there was a spark and Adren couldn't go any farther. She strained against it, but her barrier couldn't break through the fairies' one. If it were possible to say 'I told you so' by walking, she did it as she stepped back and indicated the fairy barrier.

With a slow inhale, Nadin squared his shoulders, and left their barrier to walk through the other.

Which resulted in him banging his nose against it far harder than could possibly be comfortable. Adren laughed as he danced around, hands on his face.

"It's like walking into a door!" he complained, making Adren laugh even harder. "I didn't even feel it the last time! Aw, Adren, I think I'm bleeding."

Still chuckling, Adren told him to squat so she could get a cloth out of her pack. While she did, the unicorn nickered, nose pointed at Nadin.

"Let it see the blood," Adren said. Nadin removed his hands. The flow was slow for a nosebleed, but there was enough on his upper lip to threaten drippage. With another nicker, the unicorn touched its horn to Nadin's nose. Its healing magic emanated from the horn like threads, entering

Nadin's skin with infinite gentleness. Nadin watched in awe, utterly still from that moment until the unicorn drew its horn away with a snort of satisfaction. As it did, Adren handed Nadin the cloth, which he used to clean up.

"I will never get used to that," he said.

"I wish I could see it," Adren replied. "Sorry for laughing. I never expected watching someone walk into an invisible wall would look so funny."

"It probably *was* pretty hilarious, I'll admit." Nadin stood, returned the cloth. "Time to try again."

"You can't be serious." Adren gestured at him to squat again, raising the cloth and giving it a shake. Red in his cheeks, he did, and she wrapped the cloth up carefully before returning it to the pack.

"I could go through it before, I swear!"

"Of course you could. I'm not questioning that. But it looks like a fairy followed you when you came here last time and they fixed the enchantment so it wouldn't happen again." She drew back from the barrier. Her eyes were sad, but only for as long as she faced the direction neither of them could go. "I'd hoped we'd be able to find out whatever it is the unicorn keeps running to."

"Maybe we could find a way in?"

"No, better not. If they're expecting that we might come by again, then there's no telling what other guards they have in place. And it'll be harder to bargain with them after we've trespassed on this place they're obviously putting a lot of effort into keeping safe from outsiders."

"You're going to give up?" Although Adren had started

off, Nadin's feet remained planted.

She sighed, stopping well before she was too far for her barrier to protect him. "Today wasn't the first time the unicorn's gone to something that way and met opposition. There will be other chances."

"What if this is the only place like this?"

"If I'm curious enough, I'll come back and find a way in. But, as I said: we need to be able to make a deal with the fairies. I'm not going to antagonize them with this. That would be stupid. And we're going to be smart." She grinned.

This time as they entered the fairy throne room, they had guards. They wouldn't have called themselves that—when Adren, Nadin, and the unicorn arrived, the three fairies had insisted on 'escorting' them to the monarchs. Along with that insistence, they had ordered Adren to remove the barrier, as they were not allowed inside the mound. A bid for power, Adren recognized, and one she wasn't about to concede to.

"Nonsense," she said. "The barrier stays."

"We shall not allow you to enter with it."

Adren raised an eyebrow. "Then you shall have to inform your monarchs that you could have brought the Demonic Vessel to them, but you refused because of a point of conduct."

"They determined this conduct."

"Well. We'll have to wait until the monarchs change their minds. Or carry off the Demonic Vessel with us. What think you, Nadin?"

He blinked. Helpful.

Even without his input, the guards' resistance didn't last long, and Adren caught a flash of disapproval on the faces of the monarchs as the doors to the throne room opened. They should have known Adren wouldn't leave herself exposed like that, even if she did have a part-fairy to accompany her.

"We hear you wish to make a deal with us," intoned the queen. She and the king sat on their thrones, but Iraem's was empty.

"I have considered one, yes."

On the way from the barrier, Adren had told Nadin about Denyeh's husband. The fairies weren't likely to give him up willingly but, from what she knew of the fairies, she had the feeling Denyeh's husband wouldn't be far from the monarchs. She had instructed Nadin to pay attention to everyone they passed by, and everyone in the throne room. If any lacked magic and had a spell on them instead, he would clear his throat and, when she tapped her leg, point one of his feet in the direction of the one in question. Adren had the feeling the fairies had put enough of an illusion on Denyeh's husband that none of the humans would recognize him, Denyeh especially. Why else would Denyeh have been out in the market when the fairies invaded if not to try to find her husband? How else could all the fairies have attacked the prison without any of the guards identifying their old captain?

She had also, in an attempt to avoid something like what he'd done to indicate that there weren't any fairies following both of them in town, made him practise over and over until she was certain he wouldn't make a fool of them both.

The whole way to the throne room, Nadin didn't signal. He didn't even signal by accident. But once they stood before the dais of the throne room, he did.

"Is this unicorn part of your deal?" asked the king. He disguised it well, but Adren couldn't help but notice the pause he made before the word 'unicorn.'

"No." Adren tapped her leg, and Nadin pointed to the left.

"Then why have you brought it?"

"Because it is my servant demon and I require its presence." A quick glance showed a number of fairies in that direction, including the one Adren suspected was not what he seemed. It also showed Nadin appearing sick. Not enough to be concerned about, but enough to notice. No matter. It would pass. Denyeh's husband located, Adren could now begin her real work.

The king snorted. "A demon? Only the ignorant believe in such things."

"And only fools disbelieve what they may see with their own eyes."

Under any other circumstances, Adren's words would have been treated as the height of disrespect but, though Nadin couldn't find a thing, Adren knew all the fairies saw what Iraem and Loram had. Even if no one believed the unicorn to be a demon, their imaginations could provide them with all sorts of unpleasant details. The monarchs exchanged a look, their discomfort clear.

"You may think yourselves superior to me, but I have

abilities you cannot see. In all you have done to me, in all my time here, I have never once engaged with the fullness of what I have. And yet, here I am before you, with the very thing you covet the most in my possession, and the very thing you fear most under my power. You think because you sit on thrones that you are more than I. I say you have much to learn." All technically true, but the monarchs didn't need to know in what way.

"What is it you would teach us?" asked the queen as she leaned over to put hand to chin. Evaluating Adren, was she? Well. Adren intended to make an evaluation of her own.

"Tell me," Adren said. "What would you do to the humans with the magic of the Demonic Vessel, should I give it to you?"

The queen laughed. "Does the White Changeling care what happens to them?"

"You know that answer already."

"We intend to continue our games with them," said the queen with a wave of her hand. "They think their barriers strong, and strong they may be, but we shall tear those down and deal them the consequences of breaking the rules. A story among them says a saint gave them power, but any ability they have beyond that of ordinary humans came from fae and human intermingling in ages past. We regret this and see now that it has made them arrogant. Magic is not good for humans. It twists their minds, makes them unmanageable. We shall find the remnants of our mistake and we shall solve this problem we created. After all, if one dislikes the consequences of one's actions, one must learn from them and take the appropriate steps."

Oh, gods. Gods, gods, gods.

Adren's heart sunk more and more to her gut with each word the queen said and the obvious delight with which she said it. Of all the options she had for the wooden hand, she'd leaned most to giving it back to the fairies. But it was as Denyeh had said. The animosity ran too deep.

Except the fairies had gone beyond animosity. They saw the situation as entertainment, *cruelty* as entertainment. Their reason for what they did had nothing to do with justice or seeking the good of another. Their actions had no higher purpose than laughter.

And so, while the queen talked, Adren let out some of her magic, hoping it wouldn't be noticed so close to the magic in the hand. She sent it to burn the wood. Not entirely— she didn't want to risk that—but in a line along the grain, and under her own hand so no smoke could escape. The one thing that worried her in all this was the magic in the hand. If she harmed its container, what would it do? Her memory of when it washed over her softened that concern. After all, it had listened and pulled away when she didn't want it to touch the dark place in her mind. So, as that line burned, she willed that the magic beneath it would leave to where it had come from, and that it would never again let the fairies access it. As soon as she could feel the wood on either side of the line shift, she stopped the magic, hoping it would be enough.

"As you attempted to place judgement on me, so I place it on you," Adren said when the queen finished, lifting the wooden hand at such an angle that none of the fairies could see the charred part. She spoke with care and kept her tone low. The queen drew back. The king seemed as if he'd received either a compliment or an insult, but couldn't tell which. "And I judge you unfit." With that, Adren broke the hand into two pieces.

CHAPTER
FOURTEEN

The magic escaped the hand the moment Adren broke it. It spread out and up like a tree of living glass before streaming away, its presence emptying from the throne room. All the fairies drew back, as did Nadin, but while their attention stayed on the magic, his went to Adren. Her hands shook. Enough that he could see, but no one farther than him. And it lingered even after she lowered them.

It took the monarchs a moment to process what had happened. They stared at the pieces of the hand, openmouthed. The queen understood first and rose, her movement harsh.

"Do you perceive what you have done?"

"I have taken from you that which you would have used for naught but the cause of suffering," said Adren. "An I have done wrong in this, then I shall take what I am given. But it shall not be from you."

A sly smile touched the queen's lips. "Ah, and what of the humans? We are not wholly without power and they…"

Her smile grew. "They have nothing such as we do."

"They have an army interested in the fate of the Saint's Gauntlet, as well as barriers such as the one we have. All they need do is send a protected messenger to the nearest towns to gather a greater force, both in numbers and in magic, capable of victory over you, no matter your power. They shall do this when I have told them you conspire with Breim, that I brought the Saint's Gauntlet here only for it to be destroyed, and that you have made plans to end the lives of humans." Adren said all of this carelessly, as if unaware of the steel her words contained.

"You would lie to them to cause us suffering?" At this statement from the queen, Adren gave an almost imperceptible pause. If you didn't know her, you would not have given it much thought. If you did, you would see it, and you might even notice the tension in her fingers as they curled. Nadin held his breath during that pause, only exhaling when Adren's hands relaxed and her back straightened by a hair's breadth.

"I would tell them the truth so that they may protect themselves from your selfishness. How they interpret the truth is not my business. As I recall, you used the same strategy with me."

"So *that* is your deal," said the king, sitting back in his throne. "Leave the humans unharmed and remain unharmed ourselves.

Adren raised a finger. "Close. The deal is this: any harm you inflict from this point on the humans in that town—no matter if they belong there—shall turn itself back on you in equal intensity. Accept those terms, and I shall give you the chance to regain the pieces of the Demonic Vessel, to do with them whatever you wish. Do not accept these terms, and the humans will destroy you for all your past harm against them and to protect themselves from all harm in the future."

"What choice have we? We accept. What is this chance you wish to give us?"

Here, Adren made a wide gesture. "I invite any and all in this room to break this barrier. Should you prove successful, you may take the pieces and none of us will stop you." She placed a hand on the unicorn's shoulder. It shivered under her touch, but didn't move.

With a nod from the king, the fairies sent their magic at the barrier. It throbbed with their onslaught, pulsing in brilliant colours with each attack. Not one drop of magic made it through. After a while, there was a lull, during which it became clear that one fairy had hung back behind the others and had failed to contribute to their effort.

As Adren had thought, Denyeh's husband wouldn't join in the attack. He didn't have magic. Possibly, the fairies could have sent him to retrieve the pieces of the hand, but the barrier wouldn't allow any spells they'd placed on him to come through. Even if he managed to enter the barrier, he would be free of Iraem's influence. And, Iraem being the princess, Adren doubted the other fairies would let her plaything be freed. That is, not unless she'd given them great enough cause. So it had worked, and she had found him.

The best part of all this was that Adren had been right about which one he was.

"Barsae! Why won't you come and take them? Prove your worth to your monarchs."

"She toys with you, Barsae," said Iraem, who had now entered the throne room. She went to him and wrapped her arms around his waist.

"You know, Iraem, I heard from Loram that you purposefully discredited her. That you are the reason she was taken by the humans and the Demonic Vessel was lost."

"That is a lie." One would think that kind of statement would be believed by its speaker, but no sweetness flowered on Adren's tongue. She hadn't expected it to.

"If it is, then why have you offered her no opportunity to regain her pride? Had it been your idea to leave her out of the attack on the prison? And what about leaving her to watch the children, despite a number of near-adult fairies who didn't need her help, while everyone else searched the town for the hand she lost? Shall you do the same to Barsae, should he rise too high for your liking?"

"You did convince us to treat her poorly," said Barsae to Iraem. "I wondered at that." He disentangled himself from her and made his way to the barrier. The other fairies, eyeing both Iraem and the barrier in turn, let him pass through. Adren wondered how many *other* things Iraem had done that one might wonder at.

Barsae put one hand on the barrier and pushed. His fingers went through without much resistance, and his palm and arm passed through the magic only a little slower. The rest of his body, however, made no perceptible progress. He strained against the barrier, both arms now inside, his feet sliding back every time he tried for a better angle.

The king, with a gleam of understanding, whispered to the queen and smiled. Adren held the queen's gaze, defiant, but the queen merely inclined her head.

"Nadin, help him through. Can't you see he's having a hard time?"

"Can't I..." Nadin's voice trailed off. He nodded.

As Nadin worked on the spell that held Barsae, the fairies drew back. Except Iraem. Adren could almost feel the rage flowing off her in waves.

Barsae had forced half his body through the barrier by now, and the resistance he faced grew less with each passing moment. It would not be long before he was free of whatever spell Iraem had put on him to make him forget who and what he really was.

"Um, Adren? I think Iraem's sending some kind of spell towards Barsae."

Saints.

A flash lit the room as if the sun had decided to join them. As it dimmed, Iraem gave a wordless cry, and Barsae entered into the protection of the barrier.

Nadin blinked. "The monarchs stopped it."

The monarchs... really? Adren felt a throb of hope that Denyeh had been wrong, that Adren had been wrong, that the world could right itself and be as it was again.

"Leave them be, Iraem," commanded the king. Iraem paused. "Thou hast lost this game, and we shall not support thy steps to begin another. The White Changeling has played it well and impressed us. We would not, however"—here he turned back to Adren—"suggest she play it again. Our treatment of her shall not be so gentle a second time."

That stung. She would have thought he was lying if not for the taste of honeysuckle at his words. Adren may not have been a fairy, but she still had her pride. Turning on her heel, she led the others out of the throne room, taking the pieces of the Demonic Vessel with her.

"Damn fairies," said Barsae once they were well away from the mound. Nadin grimaced, but didn't say anything.

"I take it your name isn't really Barsae?" Adren asked.

"It's Parsa, actually. How did you know I wasn't a fairy?"

Adren indicated Nadin. "He can see magic."

"And you're the White Changeling. I ought to arrest you, but I think I'll find an excuse not to, all things considered. I thought you never helped humans?"

"I thought so, too." She avoided Parsa's eyes. "Would you do us a favour?"

"Anything."

"His pack is somewhere in the prison. Could you get it back for him?" Parsa gave the pack on Nadin's back a quizzical look. "He's carrying mine right now."

"I want to know why you would need his pack from prison, but I think I won't ask."

"You can always ask your wife later. She's the one who made sure he got in there in the first place."

Parsa's eyes went round.

"It's a long story," said Nadin, earning him a raised eyebrow from Adren.

"I believe you. A lot seems to have happened while I've been away," Parsa said. He stretched. "I feel a little sorry for Iraem."

"Don't," Adren replied quickly.

"But I do. She never seemed in control of her life—always reacting, always scrabbling for power. She never had peace, living like that." He sighed. "I'm glad to be rid of her. These last two weeks have been a nightmare."

"What about the spell? That can't have been pleasant."

"Oh, it was bad. But Iraem was worse. She was the one who made it, after all."

A soft wind played through the trees. With the sun near setting, deer had come out to feed. They watched the group, alert, a few darting off with the slightest crack of a twig. Others stayed, munching leaves, at least one ear towards the interlopers at all times. A chickadee called its name and several birds took off.

"Adren! Nadin!"

Loram came after them, waving. A barrier surrounded her at about an arm's length away on all sides. Adren interrupted the enchantment for their barrier so the fairy didn't have to stand at an awkward distance from them.

"Loram?" This was Parsa.

"Oh, Parsa!" Loram pulled out a spoon. The barrier around her followed, keeping the utensil at its centre. "Tell Denyeh thank you for this!"

"A spoon?"

"An enchanted spoon." Loram grinned, putting it back into her skirt pocket. "The monarchs were furious that I helped all of you, but they couldn't do anything to me through the barrier. Of course, I can't stay here anymore—"

"Come with us," said Adren. "You'll have a place with the fairies I grew up with."

Loram gave a roar of laughter, startling the deer. She seemed about ready to dance. Instead, she adjusted her shawl. "And here I thought I only had the one choice! Thank you, Adren, but I'll be leaving with Hin tomorrow morning to stay with his people. Which is why I came. You'll be heading north when you leave, right? Then will you two join us for however long you can?"

"I was thinking of leaving once we had Nadin's pack."

"Adren!" Nadin's voice cracked.

"What? The soldiers want to put both of us in prison."

He groaned. "I was looking forward to a full night's sleep on an actual bed. In an inn."

"If you go to sleep in an inn, you might never want to leave."

"I've been dreaming of pillows and mattresses for a week. If I could have, I would have slept for days at Denyeh's house." Nadin had a faraway look in his eyes. He gave a deep, forlorn sigh.

Parsa chuckled. "If you want a night in an inn so badly, I can help you with that. I'm not the captain of the prison guards for nothing, and being kidnapped by fairies will give me pity points."

"You," said Nadin, "are my new favourite person."

Adren agreed to the idea only because she hadn't really wanted to leave right away. While she didn't mind sleeping outside, she'd still missed a lot of sleep in this whole debacle, and the attacks had kept her from a full night's rest often enough that she'd started to feel it.

Aw, who was she kidding? She wanted to stay at an inn, too.

Parsa took the lead to the prison. As he did, Adren beckoned for Loram to join her. When the fairy had fixed her shawl, it had reminded Adren of something. The two of them drew back a bit from the others.

"I have a question."

"Anything."

"It's a bit embarrassing… please don't tell anyone I didn't know the answer to this." Especially since she'd lived with fairies.

"I shall keep silent. But you intrigue me with your hesitation."

"Nadin heard you say to Iraem that she'd bared your back to someone. What does that mean?"

The corners of Loram's lips turned down. "Have you heard the stories humans tell about what the backs of fairies are like?"

Adren nodded. The day the children had told her that fairies stole children, they'd also told her how fairies had hollow backs. Or backs covered in bark. Or no backs at all. She'd thought they were making it up.

"Our backs are the one thing we can never cover with illusion. We can hide it under clothing and cast an illusion on that clothing, of course, but the moment our skin is bare, it can only be seen as it is."

"Which is?"

"Ridged. Mine can be mistaken for cedar bark, at a distance. Iraem made sure the soldiers knew I wasn't human, even if they only thought they'd been lucky and saw it before I could set an illusion. You didn't know about any of this?"

"The fairies I lived with didn't tell me."

"But surely you must have seen—"

"No. Their clothing always covered them to the neck, not like the ones here. I mean, I saw it a bit on babies and toddlers, but I thought they grew out of it." For once, the humans had gotten it right. Mostly. Imagine if they knew they had, at least in this town. The humans would all always be able to know if they were dealing with a fairy without having to rely on Denyeh's warning signals, which fairies could always tamper with. But what if that knowledge spread and humans started to use it to ostracize the part-fae living with them? What if they took what was meant only as defense and used it as a weapon? Considering all the fairies had done here, Adren wouldn't be surprised if there were humans who wanted vengeance.

"Humans shall have to know sometime," said Loram, both hands on her shawl. "We have all our magic, and what do they have? Stories and half-truths. So long as the army thinks it can get the Saint's Gauntlet, this town is protected. But now that you've broken it, the people here need something more. What better way than to give them a way to see through our illusions?"

"But what if they use that to hurt you?"

"We still have our other magic. We're not helpless, after all. Our positions would simply become more equal." She laughed. "What a thought."

For a fairy, yes.

"You know," Loram continued, "the fairies here are terrified of the humans, with their stories of saints giving them power. And I think the more we're scared of someone, the more we hide from them."

"We? Fairies?"

"Anyone."

Nadin and Adren waited in the forest just outside the prison while Loram and Parsa went in to talk to the soldiers, Parsa carrying Denyeh's enchanted spoon. Parsa hadn't thought anything would go wrong, but Adren refused to be indoors if it did. Nadin agreed with Adren.

They could see Denyeh rush, tears on her face, to meet her husband before he'd gotten anywhere near the entrance. The two embraced and kissed each other before they went around to the entrance, arms linked and hands clasped together.

"I'm so glad we found him," Nadin said.

"Me too," said Adren, at which Nadin leaned back, eyebrows raised. But Adren was smiling, her sun-through-the-clouds kind of smile.

The sky had turned red with the end of the day and, as they waited, they made themselves comfortable. Adren, who hadn't had the benefit of a nap, and who had only just managed to convince the unicorn to leave for a while, lay down and used a mossy log for a pillow. Before long, she had fallen asleep.

Nadin lasted a bit longer, sitting with his back against a tree, watching the prison intently. He nodded and snapped his head up. Nodded a bit more. Made some sort of half-hearted complaint under his breath. Nodded again. Drifted off.

FIFTEEN

Something hard shoved at Adren's shoulder. She opened her eyes. The sky had turned velvet black and full of stars. Beneath it, soldiers stood around her and Nadin, a couple carrying lamps.

"You might want to wake him up," said Parsa, indicating Nadin. He'd changed out of the fairy clothing and now wore his captain's uniform. Rubbing her eyes, Adren sat up. Nadin sat against a tree, chin on his chest and a little puddle of drool on his shirt.

She supposed she couldn't blame him.

"Nadin!" she said, with a jab to his ribs.

"No!" he said, head lolling to the side. "You have to put the porcupine on the haystack. It's the only way it can fly."

Adren smirked and got up to shake him. He opened bleary eyes.

"The colour blue and the colour green are fighting again," he said with the enunciated clarity of a child. "What are you pointing at?" When he followed her gaze to the soldiers, he started.

"We'd like to escort you to the inn," said Parsa. "As it turns out, the lord of our county has no warrant out for anyone of Adren's description and someone who stayed in town to deal with the fairies after being imprisoned couldn't possibly be a Breimic spy." He shrugged. "Who knew? As thank you, the stay at the inn for both of you is covered, but we'll have to escort you there and escort you out of town. To make sure Adren leaves without causing trouble."

"I'm confused," said Nadin. "You're using way too many words and I'm way too sleepy."

"We're going to sleep at the inn," said Adren, helping him up and grabbing their packs.

"I told you Parsa was my new favourite person."

The soldiers brought the two of them to an inn near the market, where two adjacent rooms had been made ready for them. Nadin went into his and, with a happy sigh, plopped onto the bed. He was asleep in a moment.

Adren closed the door for him and went into her room. Like Nadin's, it was clean and small, just big enough for the bed and a space for her to put her things. She pulled out her extra set of clothing from her pack and changed before slipping under the blanket and into dreamless sleep.

They both woke in the early afternoon to find a note from Loram saying that she and Hin would be waiting for them by the main road and not to hurry. It seemed she'd heard how tired they were. So, while Adren took a bath, Nadin cleaned their clothing—and the cloth he'd gotten all bloody—and hung it to dry on the inn's electric heater. He got to talking with the innkeeper about how the machine worked, which led to telling the innkeeper about Lord Watorej's motorized carts, which led to Adren having to yell for her clothing. While Adren organized food, Nadin had his bath without having to yell for anything.

Before they left, they sat in the dining area to eat. Nadin kept getting bowl after bowl of food, long after Adren had finished.

"Parsa's going to regret paying for everything," Adren commented. "You could bankrupt the entire army at the rate you're eating." She made as if to say something else, but stopped herself.

Nadin responded between bites of his fourth serving. "He should have known better. I'm still growing."

It took bowl number six to vanquish his appetite.

"So good," he said as he sat back and patted his stomach. He grimaced. "So full."

"Then it's time to get going," said Adren as she got up and shouldered her pack. The soldiers waiting for them took this as their cue and stood as well. Adren frowned.

"What?" asked Nadin.

"Later," she said. "When the soldiers are gone."

The townspeople stared as the soldiers escorted Adren and Nadin out of the town. Nadin tried to start a conversation several times, but Adren only responded with monosyllables. At the edge of the town, Nadin told the soldiers to say goodbye to Denyeh and Parsa for him. The soldiers said they would, and then waited at the edge of the town as Nadin and Adren headed out.

"Nadin—"

"Adren, Nadin! Look who joined us!"

Loram stood up from the place by the road where she and Hin had been waiting. The unicorn, spotting Adren, trotted up to her and snorted in her face. Its pleasure at seeing her danced through their connection even as Adren wiped her face of the droplets it had sprayed onto her skin. So much for that bath.

So much for talking to Nadin alone.

After greeting each other, they got off the road and settled into formation with Loram, Adren, and the unicorn in the front, and Hin and Nadin in the back. Adren wasn't sure she felt comfortable with this arrangement. She kept thinking of what Loram had said about the unicorn.

"Were you telling the truth when you said that you knew of the cure I'm looking for? The one for insanity?"

"That was for the unicorn, wasn't it?"

"Yes."

Loram took a deep breath. "Half of what I said was truth. We might have been able to cure it, with the power we had."

"The magic of the Demonic Vessel."

"Aye."

Tears burned to be released. The unicorn drew closer to Adren and she leaned against it, eyes closed and face turned from Loram.

"You care about it deeply, don't you?" Loram asked.

"I do."

"I understand you not, Adren. You act as if all you care about in the world is magical creatures, and yet you did everything in your power to understand and solve the conflict here so even the humans would be protected. I had expected you would have given me the Demonic Vessel the moment I'd removed the spell from you, bade me return to the mound, and left town then. Or simply left when Nadin returned with the Demonic Vessel partway filled with magic and used it to essay to heal the unicorn, leaving us and the humans to deal with each other. Such actions would have found applause among my kind. But you acted entirely outside of our struggles for power, and you succeeded not only for yourself, but also for all you spoke for and to." While some of this relieved the heaviness in Adren's chest, she couldn't help but think of the king's final words in the throne room.

"It only worked because your monarch played with me. Gently."

"I heard you in the throne room, and I know better. Aye, they played. All is a game in their minds. But they did not play gently. They played thinking you would adhere to their rules and you did not. Their rules keep the game ongoing. Their rules create and nurture people like Iraem. And when you chose to follow new rules, you chose those that, when followed to their natural outcome, would end all games of the kind the monarchs play. So, to hold their power, they spoke to make you fear them and shrink from any future dealings with them. Otherwise, you would destroy all that they had and valued."

"This sounds naught like the Loram I first met when I arrived in this town."

Loram smiled to herself. "Denyeh has a remarkable ability to see what others cannot."

Adren couldn't argue with that.

"I know you say you are neither human nor magical creature, and you refuse to allow us to consider you one of ours. I care not what you are, but I have seen who you are, and thou art more than all the fairies I have every known. Deny this all thou mayest, but I will not listen to thee. Thou hast my admiration, and thou shalt always have it."

The moment Loram switched to 'thou', Adren felt tears rush to her eyes. Even the fairies she'd grown up with had never addressed her that way.

"Gods, Loram." Adren gave a weak smile. "I don't want to cry right now."

"Then we shall speak of other things until we part," Loram said, putting a hand softly on Adren's shoulder.

Illusion surrounded Hin and Nadin such that Adren wouldn't hear anything the two said and wouldn't even see that they had said anything.

"Hast thou any message thou wish'st me to bring to the family? News of when thou shalt return to Breim?"

"No, nothing."

They lapsed into silence, Nadin hunched and a little pale, but not offering up any sort of explanation or apology.

"Where is thy mother?" Hin asked. "Wisheth her to be with us? I may arrange for something—"

"No, please!" Nadin said in a strained voice.

"Truly, there were whispers that some may have to find thee and her, for preparations are nearly—"

"I don't want to talk about this right now."

Hin frowned, Nadin's appearance seeming to dawn on him. "Nadin, art thou ill? Thou seem'st as though thou mayest become sick."

"If you mean what I think you mean by that, don't worry. I won't. I just... don't want to talk about this. Please." He stared at the ground.

"An thou wish'st to return, thou needest only send word and we shall have thy place for thee in a few months."

"Thank you. I'll keep that in mind." But he looked even queasier than before.

"Here is where we part," called Loram. Hin removed the illusion as they caught up to her and Adren.

"Farewell," said Adren.

Loram gave her a hug. "I thank thee. Shouldst thou ever need my help, tell me." Both Adren and Nadin froze. She let go. "Farewell, Nadin. Perhaps we may meet again. Hin, don't be rude."

"What?"

Loram inclined her head towards Adren and Nadin.

"Oh. Um. Fare you both well."

"Better. Come on." She put her hand on his back, like a mother directing an absent-minded child, and the two of them walked off.

"Good-bye," Nadin said. Loram and Hin just waved.

When Loram had hugged her, Adren had been so shocked that she didn't know what to do. When was the last time someone had hugged her? Nadin's near-crush of her lungs didn't count. As the fairies left and she and Nadin continued on their way, she kept her eyes straight ahead and hoped he didn't see her flush.

"Adren, you made a friend!" Nadin wiped mock tears from his face. "I'm so proud."

"Smart aleck," she shot back. Her skin was too light for anyone to miss her blushes anyways. As she did, she noticed how nauseated Nadin seemed.

"Are you all right?"

"I'm fine."

"If you're lying and you puke all over your clothing, I'm not helping you clean it up."

His response consisted of a grimace and a long, long silence. Well, she'd warned him.

"I'm sorry," she said.

"For what?"

"For how I've been treating you. What you said about the put-downs... I've been a jerk and you've always been decent. You were right to ask me to trust you because of your track record instead of whether or not you're human. I can't promise knowing you're part fairy won't change anything, and I can't promise anything about any other people we meet. It's all mixed up right now. But, for what it's worth, I'm sorry."

"Thanks." His queasiness paused in favour of a slow smile. "I appreciate it."

Honeysuckle.

No more words.

They travelled like that for a while, on the springy ground of the forest, each spear of sunlight warming them for a moment as they passed through. A deer, with delicate steps, approached a bush, scaring a robin in the process. The robin shot from the bush, scolding all the way, and retreated up into the highest cedar branches. Startled by the explosion of movement, the deer drew its head away and stepped back, but didn't run away. Slowly, it lowered its head again and nibbled at the leaves.

"I never knew how much I didn't know about fairies before," Nadin said. "You really didn't mean it when you said the unicorn was a demon?"

"Demons don't exist."

"Oh."

He didn't seem convinced.

Map of Evinad
by Nadin

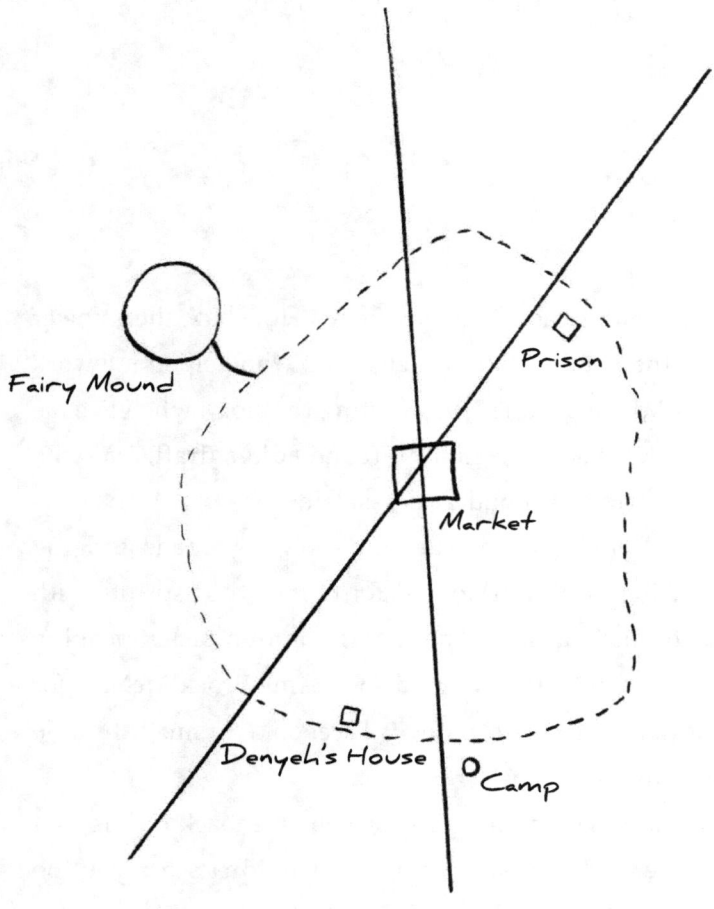

Fairy Mound

Prison

Market

Denyeh's House

Camp

ACKNOWLEDGEMENTS

The first thank you goes to Taryn Hunchak, the Knower of All the Spoilers (all of them), and who helped me work out plot details while I was writing the story, who gave me feedback for both the first draft and edited draft, and who continues to be a wonderful best friend.

Thank you so much to Lewinna Solwing for encouraging me during NaNoWriMo and for doing word sprints with me. You helped me keep on track and on task. Speaking of word sprints, thank you also to Amy Brock McNew for organizing word sprints over Facebook. So much fun. So many words.

Krista Walsh, thank you for your feedback on the first draft (yeah, I said early draft so I wouldn't scare you too much, but that really was my first draft). Having input from someone with no prior knowledge of the series whatsoever was so, so helpful for my edits later.

A huge thank you goes to EJ Clarke for being an amazing

editor (thanks to you, I now know that 'shrunk' is, in fact, the past participle of 'shrink', not the simple past like I thought). You keep track of so many details—complicated verb tense usage, in-world spellings and vocabulary, inter-book treatments of compound words, logic slips, mood usage—I don't know how you do it, and I'm grateful that you do.

This book has a beautiful cover thanks to Roberto Calas. Roberto. You put so much work into this one, and I love how it turned out. Thank you a million times over.

To Polly Olito, thank you for being awake at 1:30am to answer two quick, random questions. (Or, as you put it, "Special thanks to Polly, who was able to arbitrarily choose between a central mid-back rounded vowel and an open front unrounded one," which is a much more linguistically accurate description).

There's one person who will be reading this page before anyone else, and that is Lara Reyes, drawer of maps and paperback formatter extraordinaire. Thank you so much for your work. I don't even know where to begin to describe how much of a relief it is to have you take over these essential parts in the process of bringing this book to life.

Last but not least, thank you to God for generally being God and for specifically being around when I was certain this book was awful and broken beyond relief, reminding me that I always have this moment in every story I write and I'll probably feel better after I sleep or have something to eat. It's the little things.

ABOUT THE AUTHOR

 Thea van Diepen hails from the snowy land of Canada and that fairest of cities, Edmonton, Alberta. She is, of course, entirely unbiased, due to her Bachelor's in psychology (wait, that's not how that works...) and is obsessed with Orphan Black, Madeleine L'Engle's books, and nerdy language things.

Her website is expectedaberrations.com, home of all things that lie on the edge of the bell curve, and she can be contacted via that site, in English or French. If you do contact her in French, though, please don't ask her to count in it as she tends to skip numbers ending in six entirely by accident.

Hidden in Sealskin
Book One

(available as both ebook and paperback)

In her search for a cure for an insane unicorn, a misanthropic outlaw sets out to steal a sealskin. Things get complicated. She hates complicated.

"This story is filled with wondrous things…"
~Teddi Deppner, author of The Author Collector

Hunter and Prey
Book Three

Adren returns home to a request for help from a woman accused of being a werewolf. Meanwhile, the fairies nearby ask Nadin to find something they either can't or won't describe. This forest holds secrets, and all of them are dangerous.

Coming soon to an Amazon near you.

The Illuminated Heart

(available as both ebook and paperback)

A retelling of the Norwegian fairy tale 'East of the Sun, West of the Moon,' except in Iceland and with Norse zombies. And, woven through that, the story of a girl who struggles to trust God after the untimely death and undeath of her only brother.

"I'm a cynical, crotchety atheist and was ready with all my crotchety cynicism on starting this read.

"It melted me."
~Rachael Stephen, author of State of Flux

Dreaming of Her and Other Stories

(available as an ebook - paperback forthcoming)

An anthology of short stories and poetry, written as refreshers, reminders of what makes life beautiful. Pieces include a story of the life of a river as he discovers his true self, a poetic retelling of Daphne's flight from Apollo, and, in the titular story, a literal nightmare as a girl comes to terms with the death of her sister.

"...a buffet of exquisite bites of literary, emotional, and devotional grace."
~Bookloving Gal, Amazon reviewer

www.ingramcontent.com/pod-product-compliance
Lightning Source LLC
Chambersburg PA
CBHW060327260626
47160CB00007B/2702